WEREWOLF
PARALLEL

WEREWOLF PARALLEL

ROY GILL

KELPIESTEEN

KelpiesTeen is an imprint of Floris Books
First published in 2014 by Floris Books

The publisher acknowledges subsidy from
Creative Scotland towards the publication of this volume.

This book is also
available as an eBook

This book is also
available as an audio book

British Library CIP data available
ISBN 978-178250-054-4
Printed in Poland

This book is dedicated to all those who found the Parallel, and told me they'd like to spend a little more time there

Imagine the Earth as a spinning sphere. Imagine the Daemon World as another, occupying a fractionally different space. There was once a time the two were so close you could step from one to the other...

Not everyone was happy. Some believed a Human World of science – and a separate Daemon World of magic – was the way forward. And so, in secret, a dangerous plan was conceived to tear the worlds apart.

The conspiracy did not succeed. Instead of a clean separation, a gap was opened up between the worlds. The mages Mitchell and Astredo – human and daemon architects of the World Split plan – were drawn into this howling void, and never seen again. Their covens fled screaming into the night.

Nearly three-hundred years passed... The Human World became more rational and less magical, as the influence of its now more-distant Daemon twin receded. People stopped believing in monsters, and found new things to be scared of instead.

But Mitchell and Astredo had an unexpected legacy...
The descendents of the World Spilt conspirators –
those who saw the void and fled – were touched by a
strange Inheritance. They alone now could locate the
gap between the Human and Daemon worlds.

And as for the gap itself? Nothing stays empty forever...

The gap snatched echoes and stole reflections from
the worlds it bordered. All the leftover places, old gods
and creatures lost to time found a new home there.
And so it grew, and became a dark mixture of things
Humanian and Daemonic, all churned up into one.

It is the route by which those with the Inheritance can
pass between the Human and Daemon worlds. It is a
place in its own right.

THE DAEMON PARALLEL.

PROLOGUE

WHEN THE WEREWOLVES
WENT RUNNING

Alasdair Black was waiting for the clouds to clear. They were heavy tonight, dark and foreboding in the skies over Blackford Observatory. This wasn't what the forecast promised.

Time on the main telescope was limited, and Alasdair had to share its use with a number of other students, scientists and researchers. If conditions didn't improve, he'd miss his chance for observation, and his work would slip further behind. He supposed he could always get on with some analysis of existing data, but that was not where his passion lay. For Alasdair, the universe was a big box of secrets, and he wanted to be the one to crack it apart. Sometimes though, he felt the more he prised at it, the more stubbornly its lid remained shut.

He sighed, decided to take a break and climbed down the stairs to the little kitchen area he shared with the other students. Setting the kettle to boil, he glanced out the window to the hillside. It had been difficult enough getting up the steep road – he'd probably need a sledge to get back to his digs in the city without breaking his neck.

He leant forward over the sink, studying the snowy ground to see if a new frost was forming. A couple were out walking, hand-in-hand with a small boy who couldn't have been much more than four or five. The parents were both tall and striking, with long fair hair that reached their shoulders. Alasdair knew the hill was popular with dog owners and ramblers, but on a late night as cold as this one, it was odd to see people about, particularly with a young child and no cheerful, bounding mutt. He looked down. There weren't any unfamiliar cars in the Observatory grounds, so the family must've climbed here...

Alasdair frowned. *What were they up to?*

The snap of a switch drew him back to the kettle. He poured water into a favourite mug, stirring briskly. Clutching his hot cup, he took another glance out the window.

The clouds were clearing, revealing a full moon that lit up the hillside, turning the outlines of trees and bushes into a perfect silver etching. *Stargazing weather at last!*

He took a final glance at the intrepid family... the

man and woman had vanished. The little boy was alone! They hadn't lost him so quickly, surely?

Someone would have to go down, and check the boy was ok. Did that have to be him? His precious telescope time would be cut into. Alasdair reached for the phone to call George at reception.

A white shape dashed out from the cover of a clump of trees, green eyes flaring. It was a huge dog – like one of those white Alsatians, Alasdair thought – but too large for that, surely, too powerful...

This was more like a wolf.

A second white shape darted from the undergrowth, this one only slightly smaller, in close pursuit. The two touched noses, circled, then with heads down, *charged* towards the little boy.

Alasdair's chest tightened. He raised a fist and banged on the window. "You! Kid! Watch out! Look behind you, for God's sake –"

Whether he'd heard or not, by some miracle the boy chose to turn on the spot. He reached a hand to the dogs, who nosed him gently and brushed up against his side, tails waving proudly.

Alasdair breathed, and let out a nervous laugh. The dogs were friendly, and the boy knew them. He reproached himself. *Why had he been so scared?* It was almost as if he'd thought the dogs were going to fall upon the boy and devour him, like wolves in some old fairytale.

He shook his head to clear the thought. That solved the mystery of why the family were out on the

11

hill in the late, dark cold. Two huge energetic brutes like that must need walkies all the time! But it didn't explain where the kid's parents had got to...

Alasdair reached for the phone again and dialled reception. The boy was looking at the moon now, an expression of delight playing across his face. His stick-like arms reached up, his fingers outstretched as if to grab the shining disc from the sky.

And his arms kept on stretching, as if they were somehow getting longer. His fingers clenched in, then spread out again like claws. The shape of the boy's head was changing impossibly too, the ears becoming pointed and growing upwards, his jaw pushing and thrusting out, like it was turning into some kind of snout.

The child's fair hair sprouted madly, rushing down his back and covering his face. There was an awkward sort of tumbling fall, and the fur-covered boy landed on the ground, caught in a tangle of clothes.

Alasdair's mug smashed to the floor. Coffee soaked through his trainers, scalding his feet, but he didn't care. Breathless, he pressed his face to the cold glass, trying to drink in every detail of the bizarre scene that was unfolding before him.

The two huge dogs began to rip at the tangled bundle, paws holding folds down while powerful jaws lifted and shredded. Soon the material was ripped open, revealing a third, smaller animal – a puppy. It shook itself, gave an indignant *yip!* and stepped free of the torn clothes.

The largest wolf – *for that's what it was, there was no doubt now* – threw back its head and howled: a long, loud resonant cry. The second wolf followed suit, its voice blending eerily. The pup glanced from side to side at the older animals, then joined in, adding a higher pitched note to their collective voice. The howl rung out across the hillside, and then all three animals circled again, and raced away over the brow of the hill, out into the night.

For some moments, Alasdair did nothing. He became aware of a tinny, irritated voice. He lifted the phone to his ear.

" – I said, this is reception. What do you want?"

"There were – there were three people – three wolves –"

"Oh, so it's you, Black. Yes, I heard that din. So did half of Edinburgh. There'll be complaints, I'm bound. I've no time for these stupid student games!"

"It was nothing to do with me, George. I don't do pranks. I was worried about the boy –"

"What boy?"

"The one..." Alasdair took a deep breath and tried to steady his voice. "The one that turned into a wolf."

"A *werewolf*? On Blackford Hill? That'll be the day. Look, are you not a wee bit old to be wasting my time with fairy stories? What's the world coming to, eh?"

"I'm not sure, George." Alasdair put the phone down.

He stared at the paw tracks in the snow, shaking with excitement. "There's only one thing I can be certain about. Everything I've learned, everything I thought I knew, is wrong. And that is *most* intriguing..."

CHAPTER 1

DR BLACK AND MR GREY

The girl behind the counter gave an irritated sniff.

Any second now, she thought, *any second...* That pair are going to come bursting in, all noise and laughter and sweat, and I'm going to have to be pleased to see them. Well, I'm not going to give them the satisfaction.

She scanned around the dusty confines of Scott and Forceworthy's Music Shop. Considering how few ordinary human customers ever came to browse, it was amazing how quickly things could get out of place. The old-fashioned vinyl records got jumbled up, the sheet music hung skew-whiff on the swirly wire stands, and instruments were taken down from their clips and out of boxes, and left lying around.

People are always fiddling, and it's me who has to sort it out.

She folded her hands tight across her chest, and

16

glared at the dirty glass in the window. She had a good view of the stone steps that led up from the basement shop to pavement level on Leith Walk. She hadn't been out and scraped the ice away today – *if Cameron and Morgan slipped and broke their wolfy noses, it would serve them right...*

"Eve! We're here! We're here!"

The door clattered open, letting in a slender, round-faced boy in his mid-teens. Grassy streaks covered his face and hands, as if he'd been playing an exuberant game of rugby, but a close observer might've noticed his blue-checked shirt and jeans were clean and mud-free.

Dark hair flopped around Cameron's eyes, framing a hopeful expression. "Is there any food?"

"There better be. I've got such a hunger on," added a slightly taller, broader boy. His tangled fair hair reached his shoulders, brushing the collar of a battered black trenchcoat.

Some people might call him handsome, Eve supposed, but she wasn't sure. His features had an angular, shark-like look to them, and his green eyes were just a little too big.

All the better to see you with...

The line crept into her head, and she pushed it away. She liked Morgan, really, almost as much as she liked Cameron – even if he did have the face of a hunter. And she owed the pair so much; for taking her in, for being her friends, for helping her escape her old life...

But that didn't mean she was always going to give them an easy ride.

"And what time," she heard herself say, "do you call this?"

Cameron looked at her open-mouthed. Then he burst out laughing. "Quit it, Eve! You know last night was a Fat Moon. Dunno why you're acting like our mum."

"Eve's nothing like my mum," Morgan muttered. "*She's* proper fierce." He reddened, noticing both Cameron and Eve were staring at him. "What?"

"You have a mum?" said Eve. "Since when do you have a mum?"

"Since I was a pup. That's the usual arrangement, isn't it?"

"You've never even mentioned her –"

"Intriguing, but – increasingly off topic," ruled Cameron. He turned back to Eve. "We were always gonna be late. You know that. We had to shift back, go find our kit, head down here. What's the problem?"

"I've been by myself for hours," Eve said, feeling her throat go tight. "While you two dash about having fun. How is that right?"

Cameron shrugged. "It doesn't happen often. A race across the hillside, a howl at the moon. It's a laugh." He ducked into the side door that led to the kitchen area, and returned with a packet of sausage rolls and a giant carton of milk. He took a slurp, and passed the container wordlessly to Morgan.

"All these nights, though," she persisted. "They add up."

Cameron stuck out his fingers. "Three wolf-worthy Fat Moon nights a month, for around about a year – that makes about thirty-six days. Hey, you're right! That's about a month."

"One most excellent wolf month." Morgan stretched, and held out a palm for Cameron to smack. "Woop!"

"Honestly, the pair of you. You're so smug!" Eve's voice rang out, and the boys froze, then exchanged glances. Cameron, at least, had the grace to appear a little bashful.

"C'mon, Eve... It's not that big a deal, is it? You weren't rushed off your feet or anything. Who's been in?"

It was a cold January morning, and the shop hadn't been busy – not that Eve cared to admit it. "A woman, looking for an album by Sumo or Su-Go or someone. I said unless it came out fifty years ago, and she had a record player to put it on, she was out of luck. She didn't look pleased, but at least she went away."

"Classic deflection strategy." Cameron grinned. He settled down on the countertop, picked up an acoustic guitar from its stand and began to pluck at the strings in an idle fashion that only served to compound Eve's irritation. "Anyone else? Any proper clients?"

"A couple." Eve took a deep breath. "I'll check my notes..."

The music shop they all worked in was really just a front for a more exciting trade, smuggling goods from the Daemon and Human worlds via the Parallel: the dangerous, mixed-up realm that existed between them. Sometimes the things they bartered were ordinary, sometimes very strange and rare: it was all down to what the magic users in each world required for their own rituals and practices. So few people or daemons could leave their home world, it put those with the Parallel Inheritance – the power to world-shift – at an interesting advantage...

Cameron's grandmother had started this business, building up over many years a fearsome reputation as a skilled and often ruthless trader. Cameron had for a time worked alongside her, apparently in the role of apprentice. But when the very worst of Isobel Ives' devious schemes backfired – wrenching her out of the Human World, never to return – the business had passed to Cameron alone.

Now he was continuing his grandma's world-shifting trade, with the help of his two friends. Eve had settled into her new life with relative ease. The sudden materialisation in the shop of visitors from the Daemon World occasionally unnerved her, but, by and large, they respected boundaries: only the very worst-behaved would think to cast a predatory glance at the human customers... And besides, Eve wasn't exactly without experience in matters daemonic. She had spent most of her young life in the service of a powerful Weaver Daemon known only as Mrs

Ferguson, until Cameron and Morgan had rescued her. Although she was now safe from Mrs Ferguson's clutches, Eve had been left with a permanent reminder of the daemon's possession: she looked at least ten years older than her real age.

It suited Cameron and Morgan to have someone in the shop who appeared to be a confident, responsible adult – but there were plenty of times when Eve felt more like thumbing her nose at the world, running away and hiding...

Fixing the guitar-strumming boy with a hard stare, Eve opened a leather-bound ledger and recounted the details of another morning spent alone in the shop.

"There was a trade request from Mortlach Hairtman. He's a Cervidae. A stag-daemon." Eve stuck out her hands, thumbs touched to her forehead, and wiggled her fingers, miming a pair of antlers.

"Yeah, I know. Met them," said Cameron. "They were tricky. What did he want?"

"They're cultivating a new indoor forest, and they offer –" Eve glanced down, scrutinising her own handwriting. "Six-months' hunting rights, in exchange for a pathway-locator lodestone from the Human World – or the closest equivalent we can find."

"What do you think?" Cameron glanced across at the older boy. "Can we trust them?"

Morgan scratched his head. "Cervidae are usually pretty sound. Can't let one mad tribe put you off... What do you reckon to this 'lodestone'?

What would that be? What could we find for them that'd fit?"

"Compass maybe? Too simple? Or we could sort out a secondhand mobile, one with GPS. Those hunting rights would be worth something, traded on."

"Or we could keep them ourselves," said Morgan in a low voice, causing Cameron to raise an eyebrow. "Just an idea. What's GPS?"

"Global Positioning System?"

The blond lad shook his head.

"Tells you exactly where you are, using a satellite signal. Pretty amazing, now I think about it... Works great up here, dunno how it'd go on the Parallel, but if there's a connection to a Human World location..."

Eve studied the pair of them, rapt in discussion. *This was how they worked...* Cameron knew the Humanian world well – he'd spent thirteen years in it, before he'd ever heard of the Parallel. And Morgan understood most things Daemonic; how to sniff them out, track them, and hunt them down. Together, they found whatever the magic-users of each world wanted, and sneakily purveyed it to them via the Parallel, making sure to keep back a little something for themselves...

It was a good system, and they enjoyed what they did, but occasionally Eve found herself wondering where she fitted in.

"I sometimes think you two have too much fun."

"Can you have too much fun?" Cameron adopted a puzzled expression, and spread his palms. "How is that even possible?"

She shot him a look. "You're totally in love with your wolf-side for a start."

"Why wouldn't I be? It's the best thing that's happened to me... well, ever." Cameron's brow furrowed, and his whole face darkened. "After all that bad stuff I went through – first losing Dad, then finding out what Gran was really like – don't I deserve something good? Can't I have that?"

Morgan paused, mid-way through munching a sausage roll. "He is pretty awesome at it, you know."

"Hey. Thanks, man."

Eve rolled her eyes, fearing another outbreak of high-fives.

"You'd never know he wasn't born to the pack," Morgan continued, oblivious. "He picks wolf skills up freakish fast –"

"But it's not real life!" Eve hissed, causing Morgan to take a step back. "All that running about, chasing and howling like a mad thing. What about the things that need sorted here?" She threw her arms wide, taking in the paint peeling off the wood-panelled walls, the boxes and piles of clutter, and the doorway that led down to the equally packed damp-smelling cellar.

"I can do both, can't I?" Cameron stood up and returned his guitar to its stand. "I can help. It's not like I have to choose –"

"And what about me? Do I get a say?" She slammed the ledger shut, her voice rising. "Every day I have to come to your stupid old gran's stupid old shop... I'm stuck here, while you two go out, roaming round the Parallel, trading things–"

"But we agreed," said Cameron, his eyes wide. "The Parallel is proper dangerous. You don't know it like we do. You're too young –"

"I'm too young? I'm three years younger than you, Cameron Duffy, but you only think of that when it suits you." Eve marched right up to him – his head just about reached her shoulders – and poked a finger at his forehead, nudging him backward. "Just because Mrs Ferguson's horrible magic left me older on the outside than the inside, I'm stuck here in this musty vault, day after day – because *you* need someone who *looks* grown-up, in case some human busybody comes in – and it's not fair, it's not!"

There was a silence, interrupted only by the sound of Cameron's trainers scuffing slowly on the floor. Eve rubbed the corners of her eyes, and gave her head a quick shake. Morgan, she noticed, had moved stealthily to the other end of the shop, and seemed to have developed a sudden interest in a pile of records.

"Oh, Eve," said Cameron eventually. "You should've said something. I'm sorry."

"You could've asked. Sometimes I think it's not much better being here than when I was trapped at Mrs Ferguson's. I'm still not my own person."

"You don't mean that, do you?"

"Guys," Morgan's voice rang out. "You might wanna to save it. We've got company."

Clambering down the stairs from the street was

the largest man Eve had ever seen. A white formal coat strained to cover his body, and his face was grey and lumpy, with a massive wattle-like chin. His fine colourless hair bristled upwards in thin strands, reminding her of the mould she'd once found on a loaf of bread, forgotten in the kitchen. As the door opened, she shot a warning glance to the boys. They nodded back – all hint of disagreement forgotten.

All three knew instantly: this was a daemon.

"Don't mind me. I wouldn't wish to be any trouble," the newcomer wheezed, as he inched his way in. "Although that doorway of yours... Tut. Tut. Tut." He shook his vast head, sending his fatty chin swinging. "Most unsuitable! Very poor accessibility for the larger gentle-daemon. I shall make a note! I shall write you up! I will make a report to the appropriate authorities."

Morgan lifted his head slightly as the daemon lumbered past, then recoiled, as if scenting something rank. He moved swiftly away, over to the wall where the musical instruments hung.

"Can we help?" said Cameron, adopting his brightest voice. "Were you looking for something in particular?"

"Oh, not me. Most kind of you, young sir, most kind!" A pair of milky eyes blinked. "You should address your attentions to my colleague. He is the prime agent in this case."

The daemon moved aside, revealing a second visitor making his way down the stairs: a man in his late thirties with close-cropped thinning hair, dressed in a smart black suit. The man walked briskly up to the counter, and addressed Eve. "I want to speak to the owner, Ms Isobel Ives. Come on, girl. I don't have all day."

"I'm afraid she's away on business." Eve spoke calmly, using the well-practised words she had devised with her two friends. "But I'm in charge, and her grandson's here," she indicated Cameron. "Perhaps we can help?"

"I'd better introduce myself. I'm Dr Alasdair Black, and my colleague is Mr Grey."

"That figures," Morgan said sourly, eyeing the puffy-faced daemon.

Dr Black ignored him. "Let's cut to the chase. I'm not interested in purchasing any of this... this detritus, this clutter." He dismissed the contents of the shop with a wave of his hand.

There was a loud rude-sounding *paaaaarp*, and Morgan lowered a trumpet from his lips. "For sure? Some of it is pretty awesome. Makes good sounds?"

"Morgan!" Eve remonstrated. She put a hand over her mouth to stifle a giggle. "Be sensible."

"Most amusing," said Dr Black, in a tone that suggested he found it anything but. "I don't think you'll be laughing soon. You see, I've been conducting some research. It's amazing how many important documents become public over time. Even wills lodged with Daemonic law firms. And you know what? This cosy little establishment, this music-shop-that-isn't-a-music-shop..."

Eve looked up, meeting Dr Black's gaze.

"Yes, I know all about your smuggling between the worlds." The corners of his mouth were raised in the tiny semblance of a smile. "This shop, you see, it was left to Isobel Ives under certain conditions... Mr Grey, if you would?"

"With pleasure." Grey's arm snaked into his coat and drew out a yellowed parchment. He unfurled the document, and handed it to his colleague.

"The shop passed to this lad's grandma," Dr Black gave Cameron a disapproving look, "let us see... a *surprisingly* long time ago. Yes, she must've been a remarkably young woman at the time – and latterly a very, very old one."

"What can I say? I've got good genes." Cameron's face was blank, giving nothing away.

"And it was to remain hers for the duration of her life. Those were the conditions. After that it passes to whoever is Messrs Scott and Forceworthy's closest surviving relative – in this case, a Miss Dinwiddie of Burntisland." Dr Black rolled the parchment and handed it back to Mr Grey. "Have we located Miss Dinwiddie?"

"We have, sir."

"And is she well?"

"She is in rude health for an elderly lady, sir. She keeps company with many small dogs and parrots."

Dr Black's left eye twitched. "How unsanitary."

"I'm pleased to say I left her a little less cluttered." Grey ran a sausage-like finger along his gums, and puffed out. A strange sickly odour, like mushrooms cooked in sugar, hung in the air. "It's a great skill of mine. To *absorb* problems. To remove that which gets in our way." His milky eyes turned to Eve.

Cameron stepped over to join her behind the counter and she shot him a grateful glance. "Lucky old Miss Dinwiddie, eh?"

"Yay Dinwiddie. Go her." Morgan pumped a mocking fist in the air, and moved to stand on Eve's other side.

"So she gets the shop when Gran is gone," said Cameron. "What's that got to do with us?"

"You mean to tell me Ms Ives is still about? Seriously?" Dr Black spoke with heavy sarcasm. "For such an important personage of the Parallel, is it not strange no one has seen her for... about a year, isn't it, Mr Grey?"

"Indeed, sir."

Cameron paled. Eve knew he feared someone might find out his gran had left the Human World under strange circumstances – and what that could mean for the life the three of them had built together...

"We saw her... only yesterday," he said firmly. "Isn't that right?"

"That's what I remember." Beneath the desk, Eve gave Cameron's hand a tiny squeeze.

"Large as life and twice as grumpy." Morgan folded his arms, and gave one of his broadest grins, exposing long white teeth. "So you'd better go, hadn't you?"

Dr Black's eye twitched again. He leant forward and began to arrange the pens that were scattered on the desk into lines. "I have a dislike for inexactitude. I have a lack of tolerance for things that don't add up, wouldn't you say, Mr Grey?"

"Oh, a positive distaste for it." The fat man breathed heavily, sending another gust of sugary-mushroom air into the room.

"That doesn't matter." Cameron set his jaw. "You can't prove anything."

"Not to the human authorities, maybe. But the Court of the Parallel will take a different view." Dr Black buttoned his suit jacket, and turned on his heel. "Serve them, Mr Grey."

"With pleasure, sir." Grey's fat fist clenched and unclenched, cradling his wobbly chin as if deep in thought. "You are ordered to appear at the Court of the Parallel in three days time: there to produce Isobel Ives, or else forfeit the premises of Scott & Forceworthy, and all business conducted therein."

With a violent wrench, Grey pulled his hand down to chest level. To Eve's disgust, his chin stretched too, like a dollop of dough; longer and longer, until finally the section he was holding onto detached from the underside of his face. The grey flesh quickly puckered over, and he dropped the separated chin-lump with a slap onto the counter.

"Ewww – what *is* that?"

"My calling card!" The now very-slightly-less-fat Mr Grey turned and waddled towards the door. "And if you ignore its summons, you shall hear its call... Oh yes, you shall hear it. Good day, Sirs, Madam. Good day."

The three friends stared at the lump. Stuck to the countertop, it seemed to be faintly pulsing, almost as if it were breathing.

"His awful breath... That dreadful man. I've got to get rid of that thing." Without pausing to think, Eve scooped up the lump. It squirmed beneath her fingers, and she swallowed hard. As she neared the open door, she drew back her hand to hurl the lump into the street.

"Oh gross! It's suckered on!"

Frantically, she went through the action of throwing again, but the lump held fast.

"I don't think you can get rid of it like that." Morgan touched her shoulder, and indicated the desk. "You're gonna have to put it back where he left it."

Eve held out her arm and the grey lump slowly *glopped* from her fingers back to its place on the counter, where it squatted damply, like a malevolent frog.

"Ok then..." Cameron glanced at his two friends, and gave a tiny, forced smile. "No big deal. All we've got to do is figure out how to whistle up my crazy gran from the hellish void she vanished into, save the business – and get rid of that thing."

CHAPTER 2

LIKE A WOLF IN
THE NIGHT

Black paws on white snow...

The ground beneath your pads is hard and crisp.

Easy to slip on, so claws spread wide, but it's firmer than the deeper drifts – more of a kickback from your hind legs – so you can go swift.

Ears twitch, eyes scan: left to right, down to the ground, then back to the horizon. White wolf to your side, almost in camouflage with the snow, but you scent-see him – know him – instantly.

Jaw open, lips taut and drawn-back, but teeth not exposed – a wolf smile.

Morgan.

You blink, and you both understand what that means. You run together. Heart pounding, sweet night air singing through your chest. Your feet dance, and you cover miles, racing through the trees.

This is what it means to be alive.

You draw in scent, and information leaps inside your mind. Every tiny trace is a keynote of the whole it comes from. *Like icons on a computer desktop*, your human-self thinks: *each a link to something bigger.* You know that stags have passed this way, other wolves too. A mile distant, a wild boar slumbers in fusty sleep, while above you a bird of prey circles. The forest exists in your mind as a brilliant landscape: not just of what is here now, but what has been, and what is on the way.

A new scent darts in: vibrant and sharp, it demands attention. It combines a *sticky mess of cobwebs* and the *sour stink of death*, and it approaches – fast.

A pinching, prickling sensation shoots down your spine. Your hackles rise –

With a noise halfway between a cry of alarm and a wolfish yelp, Cameron came to his senses, and sat up, bed sheets tumbling from his chest.

The bedside clock glowed a blue 06:00 AM. He was in his room, in his gran's old house on Observatory Row. He frowned and patted the midpoint of his shoulders, touching the place where a clump of hair had started to rise in his dream, convinced he would find something amiss, but felt only ordinary human skin. The last night of the Fat Moon had passed, and there would be no more wolf-shifts for a month – somehow he was already dreaming of it.

Part of him wanted to lie down, roll over, and go back to sleep but the prickling sense of unease had stuck with him, and he couldn't shake it. Something was wrong. He lifted his head and sniffed.

Death and cobwebs.

Human senses were dull and vague compared to those of his wolf-self, but he could still identify a presence: something unusual and unpleasant lurking in his room.

Fully alert now, he scanned the darkened surroundings: detecting and dismissing the familiar outlines of bookshelves, mounds of clothes, his precious guitar, the boxy shape of its amp, his stereo...

Over by the window, two red dots shone like standby lights on a TV. There was no reason for them to be there, high up on the curtain. He leant forward, eyes narrowed against the half-light.

The red dots grew, and the curtain behind shifted – the material twisting and moving as if manipulated by an unseen force. A central section billowed out then hardened, taking on the shape of a spidery body. All around it, the outlines of eight legs rose up, twitching, and began to pull themselves free.

A Weaver Daemon!

Cameron opened his mouth to shout a warning, but the sound that came out was a full-bodied growl. He leapt from the bed.

The red eyes of the fast-forming daemon flared – its scrabbling legs froze.

"Didn't think I'd see you, did you?" Cameron snarled. "Didn't think I'd notice? Well, I'm no naïve kid. Not any more –"

He tore at the upper corner of the curtain, aiming to pull it from the rail, drop it to the ground, stamp on it – anything to prevent the intruder from completing its materialisation – but the material slashed instead. Four parallel lines razored across the surface, following the path of his fingers, and tracking fast towards the daemon. Two half-formed legs fell twitching to the ground, the slash marks stopping just short of the creature's body.

The daemon screeched and flailed, but Cameron paid it no heed. He whipped his hand away and stared. His fingers were thick with black fur, the nails in the shape of claws – *his hand was halfway to becoming a wolf paw.*

"Cameron... What's going on? Some of us are trying to –" Eve's voice was thick with sleep. She groped towards the light switch – then she saw the daemon. She shrank back against the wall. *"Mrs Ferguson!"*

Cameron shoved his hand into the pocket of his grey joggers, and tried to act nonchalant despite the adrenaline racing through him. "Don't worry. I dealt with it. I scared it off."

The creature's six remaining legs were curling in, rejoining the material they had grown from, its body deflating like a punctured football. Soon the curtain smoothed and hung flat once more. The last thing to vanish were its eyes, which dwindled, grew dim and merged into the flowery pattern of red and black poppies.

"*Knew* something was up." Morgan lurched in, his tangled hair half over his face. "I could sense it –"

He collided with Eve, who gave a tiny shriek. She turned, saw who it was, and punched his arm.

"Why don't you use your super senses to check where you're going?"

"Hey!" Morgan pushed his hair back, and peered at her blearily. "I'm doing my best. This is all too *morning* for some of us."

Eve ignored him, and moved to examine the curtain. Yellow streetlight shone through the slash marks. "Mrs Ferguson... after all this time. I thought she was gone for good."

"She is. We watched her burn," Morgan said firmly. "Must've been another Weaver. They can all work mojo like that – magic any bit of thread to whistle up a body. What do you reckon, Cam?"

Cameron shook his head. Now the daemon was gone, his concern lay elsewhere. In his pocket, his fingers rubbed together in a tightly balled fist. *Were they still furry? Or was that just the fleecy lining of his pocket? And how could he have part-shifted? How was that even possible, outside a Fat Moon?* He had felt *so angry* when he caught that thing creeping in...

He took a deep breath and steadied his voice. "I don't think it was her. I don't understand how it could be."

"How did you scare it off?" Eve said.

"I ripped the curtain. I tore it with..." Cameron's fist unclenched, with a sensation like muscles unknotting. Slowly he pulled it out his pocket and risked a look.

It was a normal human hand.

He swallowed. "I tore it with a pair of scissors. The Weaver hadn't fully formed. It wasn't expecting to be noticed, and I reckoned: get rid of the medium – get rid of the monster."

"Good thinking, mate." Morgan padded over, prodded the strips of curtain on the ground with his foot. Without the influence of the Weaver Daemon animating them, they were spidery legs no longer – just curls of material. "That's got to hurt... Nice one!"

Eve looked at Cameron. She'd spotted the way he'd stared at his hand. Her eyes ran over the desk, glancing at the scatter of coins, guitar plectrums, odds and ends. She picked up a small pair of scissors. "With these? They don't look sharp enough."

Cameron shrugged. "What can I say? I never liked those curtains."

There was a pause, then Eve nodded. "Hmm. Thank you for getting rid of it, anyway." She put the scissors down. "I wonder what it wanted?"

"Opportunity," said Morgan. "Wouldn't be the first time we've had a run in with the Weavers... Maybe it fancied a look round to see what it could grab."

"Makes sense." Cameron thought back to when

he'd first met Eve and Morgan. His gran had been involved in a bargain with the Weaver Daemon known as 'Mrs Ferguson', who at that time had been Eve's captor. Nothing involving Gran had ever been simple – all her plans had devious twists – and both she and Mrs Ferguson delighted in double-crossing each other. Now both of them were gone, it was all too possible other Weavers might come hunting for the magical apparatus Isobel Ives had sneakily acquired from her rival...

"Why now?" said Eve. "That's the thing that's bothering me. Why did it appear tonight?"

"I told you," said Cameron. "I was asleep. It didn't expect to be seen."

"No, no, no. You're asleep every night – well, maybe not wolf nights – so what made this night special?"

"I don't follow."

"Listen – all the time I've been here, living with you pair, I've felt safe. For the first time I can remember, I haven't had to check the shadows, or keep a lookout for eyes watching in the dark." Eve shuddered, and drew her robe tight around her shoulders. "What's changed?"

Morgan stuck his hand up the side of his rumpled Nirvana t-shirt and scratched idly. "I expect the wards have gone." Cameron and Eve stared at him. "What? You don't think I hang out here just for your sweet tempers and good looks? Cam's grandma was a serious player on the Parallel with her wheeling and dealing. Old lady would've set up *protection*."

"I'm extremely lovable and good natured, as you

know," said Eve in a syrupy voice. She lifted Cameron's guitar from its stand. "Assuming you don't want me to break this over your head, would you please tell us – *what's going on?*"

"Ok, ok! No need to be scary! You seriously never thought about this? And I reckoned you two were smart." Morgan held his hands wide and grinned. "Old Nan Ives, for all she was mad-crazy, she wouldn't have left herself vulnerable. She would've had something to watch over her home, keep intruders away. That's what 'wards' are – a protective charm. Nice bit of boundary magic, if you can afford 'em."

"And now she's gone they're breaking down." Cameron sat down heavily on the bed.

"So we might get all sorts of daemons trying to sneak in…" said Eve.

"That little curtain-mugger was probably just the first." Morgan shrugged. "Nothing lasts forever, does it?"

"I sort of hoped it would." Cameron put his head in his hands. "But it's all falling apart: Dr Black and Mr Grey at the shop, asking questions, demanding we show them Gran even when they know we can't… And now we're in danger here too. I thought we were doing all right! I thought I had fixed things."

"Oh, cheer up, mate! Might never happen."

"At least you're still a big strong werewolf," added Eve with a little smile.

"Yeah, *brilliant.*" Cameron remembered his wolf claw tearing at the curtains. That was something else he couldn't explain, another thing that seemed to be slipping out of control... He pushed the thought away. "Morgan, where would the wards be? Let's see if we can do something about that for a start."

"Well, I'm no expert, but I'd try..." The wolf-boy pointed to the ceiling. "Up?"

The trap door inched open and Cameron stuck his head into the loft. He sneezed. "Remind me again... Why do I have to go first?"

"The ladder is clearly only fit for one person," Eve called from the landing. "It's got nothing at all to do with the attic being vile and filled with mice and spiders."

"That's what I thought." Holding his torch between his teeth, he flipped the hatch all the way back, propped his hands either side of the opening, and hauled himself into the murky space.

Cameron had never been into the loft before – he'd just lifted the trap, slid stuff in and hoped for the best. He shone his torch into the gloom. The space was just as packed with tea-chests, boxes and old suitcases as he expected. Gran had been a hoarder. His dad had been too... He shook his head. He'd have to watch himself. *Must run in the family.*

"What about you, Morgan? What's your excuse?"

"Hatchway's too narrow for my shoulders. You're the obvious choice for Operation Attic."

"Yeah, yeah." Cameron swung the torch. The arc-light reflected off a sharp-toothed leer and a raised set of claws, and he let out a startled YAAARK!

"What's wrong?" The ladder rattled as Eve raced up. "What's the matter?"

"It's ok! I've found an old roommate. Can you believe it? I shoved him up here the first chance I got."

Eve regarded the glassy-eyed stuffed mongoose with disgust. "Your gran had strange notions about decorating."

"She had strange notions about everything. That wasn't the half of it," said Cameron. "Be glad she's not here any more."

Eve pushed her dark hair back from her face and gave him an odd look. "About that – I might have an idea how to tackle the Court of the Parallel."

"Oh really? What?"

"Just something that occurred to me about your gran. Tell you properly later. I'll need to find –"

"Hey, hey. What's going on? Everyone ok?" With an eruption of dust, Morgan forced his way through the hatch.

"Looks like 'the shoulders' made it after all," Eve whispered.

Cameron grinned. "Doing fine, mate. Why don't you help us look for the wards now you're up? What's it doing here anyway?"

"Got to be above all the doors and windows that need protected. Above the chimney too, if you've got an open fireplace." Morgan brushed himself down.

"Could be worse, eh? We could be clambering over the roof."

Cameron aimed his torch above his head and ran the light along the underside of the rafters. Hanging on a length of yellowed string was a stone disc about the size of a large coin. A design had been carved into the front showing a two-faced man. From under a mass of stylized curls, one proud nose pointed left, the other jutted right. A jagged crack ran straight across the middle.

"That's it. And it looks broken to me." Morgan stepped nimbly across the beams, reached up and snagged the disc. The string snapped and it dropped into his hands. He turned the disc over and examined it. "There's something written on the back..."

"Let me see." Eve studied the engraving. "It's Latin. It's quite simple. It says:

THIS TOKEN GUARDS ALL PORTALS OF THE DWELLING PLACE OF ISOBEL IVES, FROM DAY OF ISSUE UNTIL ONE YEAR AFTER SHE DEPARTS THE HUMANIAN REALMS."

"Eve, you *are* amazing," said Cameron. "How did you know that?"

"You don't work for a daemon for years without picking up the occasional dead language." She gave him a haughty look, but he could tell she was secretly pleased. "It's signed:

BY THE ORDER OF JANUS."

"Janus!" Morgan whistled. "That's a pretty classy

ward. He's *only* the Ancient Roman God of Entrances and Exits."

"Do you know him?" said Cameron.

"By reputation. He's got a bit of a connection to the pack. I might be able to lean on it. No promises."

"Do we need to go to *Rome* to get the wards fixed, and make us safe?" Eve was full of enthusiasm. "The only thing I ever liked about Mrs Ferguson was she used to play opera. I've always wanted to see Italy..."

"Nah, you're all right. No opera necessary," said Morgan. "We can catch Janus here in Edinburgh. On the Parallel."

"What's he doing there?" Cameron laughed and held up a hand. "No, don't tell me. It wouldn't be the strangest –"

"Oh, don't be dull, Cameron," Eve interjected. "The Romans got everywhere. It'll make an interesting trip."

"Hold up." Morgan gave Eve a hard look. "Who said you get to come? There's no guarantee Janus'll help. He's meant to be a right Roman pain in the –"

"I am *so* coming. You just try and stop me." Eve's eyes gleamed, and she took herself on a little dance, jumping from beam to beam. "And I know how to tackle the Court of the Parallel too – I'm the only one who does – but I'm not going to tell you how until *after* we've been."

Cameron and Morgan exchanged looks.

"You'd better say yes, mate." Morgan cast a wary

glance at Eve's clodhopping footsteps. "If she carries on like that she'll have half the ceilings down."

Cameron sighed. "You realise this is blackmail, right?"

"Is it?" said Eve. "How sweet of you to notice."

CHAPTER 3

ON THE PARALLEL LINE

The Parallel ran through the world like a geological seam – at least that's how Cameron always imagined it – a deposit of myth and madness and monsters, drawn in from the bordering Human and Daemon realms.

He remembered the first time he'd heard about it, late one night in the kitchen on Observatory Row, not long after he'd moved in. The loss of his father had been recent, and he'd felt very raw and empty. His gran had seen that emptiness, and for reasons of her own, offered up the story of the Parallel.

She had told him about the mages Mitchell and Astredo, and their bold plan to separate the Human and Daemon worlds. She told him how the plan had gone wrong, creating an inter-world gap instead. In time, the gap became the Parallel, and the descendents of Mitchell and Astredo's covens found themselves drawn back to it, and able to use it for their own ends. They alone could travel into the Parallel, and between the worlds.

"People like you and me, Cameron," Gran had calmly revealed, changing his life forever.

He'd hardly dared believe her, but with typical ruthless efficiency she had soon found a way to catapult him in. It wasn't long before he was world-shifting: slipping from the Human world to the Parallel and back again, swift as a thought. All he had to do was concentrate on a certain tune – hear it in his mind – and reality about him would change.

Everyone with the Inheritance had their own way of finding and accessing the Parallel: it came from inside, from who they were. His gran had heard music too, although her tune had been as complicated and twisted as she was. Cameron's song was direct: it strummed and surged its way forward, like a joyous riff on a guitar.

Basically, it *rocked*.

And now he was going to share the Parallel with Eve. He knew she had gone through a lot with Mrs Ferguson – things she wouldn't talk about even now – but in an odd way, the evil old Weaver had protected her as well. None of the daemons that came seeking favours from her mistress would ever have dared harm Eve, for fear of reprisal. Out on the Parallel now, though, all bets would be off...

Cameron hoped she was ready.

"This used to be a railway. They shut it down, the weeds grew over the tracks and it went wild. Got turned into cycle paths eventually." Cameron looked up from his map. "I *think* this is the right junction."

"Foxes and badgers running along lines instead of trains... imagine that." Eve seemed wistful for a second, then she shuffled her feet on the frosty ground.

They were in a raised-up area by a red sandstone wall. A line of benches was arranged around a dilapidated stone block salvaged from a fountain. An inscription round its base read:

WATER IS NOT FOR MAN ALONE.

Below them, the cycle path ran in a straight line between high banks covered in grass and trees. Cradled in an enclosure of vegetation, they were just a short distance from the bustle of the city, but it felt like they were miles away.

"So why here for a God of Entrances and Exits?"

"Morgan said Janus was a God of Journeys too, so I guess an old railway line fits. There's always some kind of link between the Human World and the Parallel."

"Doors *and* journeys. Of course," Eve said tartly. "Why didn't I think of that?"

"You start a journey by going through a door, so it's not totally mad."

Eve pulled a face. "Anything else? God of Jam, perhaps? God of Thursdays? Or would that be too obvious?"

"He's a God of January."

"Well, that at least figures." Eve banged her hands together against the cold. "Whoever he is, I hope he can fix the wards so we can get through a night without unexpected daemons popping in..."

"Worried about missing your beauty sleep?"

"Hardly. I think that's more your concern." Eve arched an eyebrow. "Your need is greater."

"You wound me," said Cameron, patting his chest. "Wards first, so we've got a secure base to work from, yeah? Then we can see about tackling Grey and keeping hold of the shop... Any chance you might share your cunning plan for the Court?"

"I'm a Girl of Mystery. I shall choose the right moment. Which is not yet."

He stole a glance at her. Even after a year, her 'new' appearance sometimes surprised him: a tall, slender woman with long black hair, not exactly pretty, but with a strong, animated face. She looked like she was in her late teens or maybe early twenties, even though he knew the spiky personality inside was a good deal younger. When she had first come to stay at Observatory Row she'd had almost nothing, and had been forced to rummage about in Grandma Ives' stuff for things to wear. She'd looked kind of mad,

47

dressed up in a ragbag of clothes... *but maybe not so much now.*

He frowned. Actually, she looked all right. When had that happened?

"Nice, um, jacket," he said cautiously. "It suits you."

"Thanks. I've had it for months." She sighed. "You really are a *boy*, aren't you?"

Cameron blinked. "Last time I checked. I was only trying to be nice."

"It doesn't matter." She shook her head. "Where's Morgan got to?"

"He had to fetch something. Something he said might be useful. He said he'd meet us by the fountain."

"Well, you may have to use a pick and chip me from the ground, for I shall shortly become a block of ice."

"Nah. I thought I'd leave you here, to puzzle future archaeologists." He studied her face for a hint of a smile. "You can always go back to the shop."

"With that grey lump stuck to the counter? No fear." Eve grimaced. "I said I wanted to come, didn't I?"

"You made a strong case for it." A thought struck Cameron. "Eve, are you ok? About world-shifting, I mean? It's just if you need –"

"*Look out!*" Her arm snaked out and shoved him into a bush, just as a motorcycle roared from the path in a blur of chrome. It sped past, circled twice around the fountain, and came skidding to a halt.

"Woo-hoo!" A familiar long-haired figure staggered off the rear of the passenger seat, shook out

48

his greatcoat and gave the driver a hearty slap on the back. "That bike is *made* of win."

Cameron pulled himself to his feet, spitting dried leaves from his mouth. "Yes, thanks for almost squashing us."

"People should watch where they're going." The driver flipped his visor, revealing a hard, blunt-featured face that glared a challenge. "Little wolf cubs should too."

Cameron bristled, and the muscles in his chest tightened. "Oh yeah? You shouldn't even be riding that thing. This isn't a road."

There was a moment of silence broken only by the purr of the bike's engine. Morgan shot a glance from his friend to the biker and back again.

"Cycle path, isn't it?" the biker said. "This is a cycle. So it's allowed."

"But strangely it doesn't say 'idiot path', does it?" Eve crossed her arms and stepped neatly between the biker and Cameron. "And yet here you are."

Within his helmet slit, the biker's eyes narrowed, as if he suspected he'd been insulted but couldn't quite work out how.

"Anyway..." said Morgan in a placatory tone, "Ta for the lift, Grant. It's appreciated."

There was another pause and Grant the biker grunted. He pointed a leather-gauntleted finger at Morgan. "I know my duty. You should think about yours, once in a while. And you–" The finger swung to target Cameron. "I reckon I'll be seeing you around, cub."

The visor snapped down, the engine revved and the bike sped off, heading away from the path and into town.

Eve waved a hand in front of her face, clearing away the exhaust fumes. She coughed. "Who is your delightful friend?"

"Why? Fancy a date?"

"Not in a million years."

"Nah, didn't think so." Morgan gave Eve his broadest grin. "He's just a dog from the pack. No one special."

Cameron had so far had little to do with other werewolves, apart from Morgan. While his friend was 100 per cent pure Were, born to the pack, Cameron's own wolf-side was the result of a desperate gamble. In the life or death struggle that had dispatched his gran he had survived only by begging Morgan to bite him, and so pass the wolf-power on. Cameron knew the pack took a dim view of humans who were recruited this way, believing they were a liability because they so rarely managed to master their baser wolfish urges. In fact, the pack didn't approve of *anything* that might call attention to the existence of Were-kind in the human world.

For the past year, while coming to terms with his new powers, his strategy had been to keep his head down and try to avoid being noticed. But Grant the biker dog had seen through that – he'd sensed what Cameron was at once.

"I thought you didn't bother with those losers

anymore?" He shot Morgan an irritated glance. "Why were you hanging out with him? And how did he mean, 'duty'?"

"Needs must. Got to show my muzzle now and again. Especially if I want a favour." Morgan yanked up his socks and tightened his bootlaces. "Look at me! I'm all shook up, thanks to that bone-rattler."

"Rattler! You said it was great a second ago."

"Got me here quicker, didn't it?" The wolf-boy straightened up. "Right, shall we do this?"

Cameron nodded. "I'm ready if you are."

"I've been ready *ages*." Eve closed her eyes, and tapped her foot, her lips moving slowly.

Interesting, thought Cameron, *she hears music too.* His own hand was moving by his side, searching for chords on the fretboard of an imaginary guitar. The song of the Parallel rocked through his mind.

Morgan lifted his nose and scented. "Ah... can't miss that Parallel smell of magic and monsters –"

Reality changed, as they shifted through.

The fountain swivelled, the crumbling sandstone blocks becoming whole as the missing sections corkscrewed out of the ground. The lettering on the side expanded, new words searing themselves into the stone with a flourish as a jet of clear liquid spouted from the top.

On the path, the vegetation shrank back and the concrete vanished. The ground trembled and split as railway tracks rose out of it, like dinosaur ribs being pushed to the surface. A building assembled in a flurry of bricks: a stationhouse with a peaked roof and a sign that read:

PARALLEL LINE

Above the doorway, a disc-shaped logo showed a two-faced man in silhouette.

A railway on the Parallel! Cameron grinned, unable to help himself. There was always something new and different to discover. That was why he loved being able to world-shift.

Eve looked pleased too, and ran over to investigate the station. He opened his mouth to call out, but as the Parallel stabilized and the song faded in his mind, he heard the eerie howl of a wolf.

He whipped round, scanning the landscape – the smart station, the gleaming tracks, the shrubs around the fountain. He could spot no one apart from his friends.

"What's up, mate?" Morgan was alert and by his side. "What's wrong?"

"Didn't you hear it? A wolf howl?"

Morgan shook his head. "Not a hoot."

"But you must've! Have you gone deaf?"

Morgan studied Cameron with a mixture of curiosity and concern. Then he sighed. "You're kind of snappy today, Shorty. You need to take a few deep breaths, get a grip –"

"I'm fine, I'm in control –"

A vision flashed into his head, of a wolf-claw slicing across bedroom curtains... Cameron glanced at his hands, but they were – of course – completely normal and human. His shoulders slumped. "Sorry. I'm imagining things. Must be. I'm probably still a bit worked-up after your biker friend –"

"Forget it. Grant's a moron."

"A big moron."

"Alarmingly big. Like a mountain. You should pick your fights a bit better." Morgan looked away, then added in an undertone, "Cool bike though."

"*Knew* you liked it."

"Bikes are boring!" Eve announced from the station entrance. "Come and look at this!"

The platform beyond was well kept, with a bench and row of plants. A steam engine in red and gold livery stood waiting, the logo of a two-faced man embossed upon its side, and the door to its rear carriage ajar.

Lying across the path to the train was a marble statue of a sleeping lion, its chipped muzzle pressed flat to the tops of its paws. A peaked stationmaster's cap rested at a jaunty angle on its head.

"Daft place for a statue." Eve reached for the cap.

"I wonder who put it there?"

"I wouldn't touch that," Cameron cautioned, stepping over the paws of the beast. "Not until we know how this place works. We might have to barter for entrance or something –"

"Oh nonsense. It's just a hat on a stone cat. There's no one about." She popped the cap on her head, crossed to the open carriage door, and struck a pose. "Would you care to board? First, second and third class tickets are available..." She raised an eyebrow in Morgan's direction. "Some of us may have to travel in the guard's van."

There was a grating sound like something heavy being dragged, and a smell of fresh chalk dust. Below Cameron's feet, the shape of the shadows changed, as if a very large object was now blocking the light. He turned around.

The statue was standing up.

It shook its mane, with a noise like a load of paving slabs being crashed together. Even in motion its flesh had a marbled quality: muscles standing out in stony rivulets along its flanks.

"This is *my* station." The creature prowled forward, its joints grinding, forcing the trio to scatter. "I decide who boards."

Eve squeaked. "I didn't realise you were alive! I meant no harm." She snatched the hat off her head and held it out. "Nice... kitty?"

"*Lion* is the word you are searching for," said the creature. Flecks of gold quartz flashed in its eyes.

54

"And I'm not sure I am nice. Now, if you'd all be good enough to stand still, I can decide what order to eat you in." Its jaws opened and a collection of tiny hard spherical objects rattled to the ground and rolled away across the platform.

Ok, thought Cameron, *a stone lion has stone drool. That makes a mad sort of sense.*

Morgan tensed. He was checking out the exits, gauging whether they could make it past the lion and onto the train, or off the platform and along the rails, or back through the station. With a slight shake of his head, he indicated now was not the time to run. Cameron silently agreed; they had no idea of the speed and agility of the creature. If its temperament was anything like that of a domestic cat, a sudden move might even cause it to pounce...

Better try and bluff it out.

"We're here to see Janus. You've got to let us on the train." Cameron spoke with a conviction he didn't really possess. "We need to get a new ward to protect our house –"

"And the girl-woman needs a heart, and your dog-friend could use a brain. Tell someone who cares." The lion yawned, letting more pebble-drool hail down. "Janus won't see just anyone. I can't let every random board the January Express." Its chest puffed importantly. "There's got to be a limiting factor – and that's me."

"The Limiting Lion?" Morgan gave a crooked grin. "Catchy name."

"It's not my name, it's a job description!" the lion roared. A fresh torrent of stone drool cascaded from its jaws, rolling like marbles across the ground. "And it's better than my sister got, abandoned underwater for 2000 years, so have a care! I'm a creature of importance!"

Cameron swiftly drew from his pocket the cracked disc they'd found in the attic. He held it up, acutely aware his reach extended only to the base of the lion's chest. "Look – Janus's token. This is his magic, his name – that must give me some rights?"

"This is his sigil, certainly. But are you the 'Isobel Ives' named?" The lion lowered its muzzle and peered. The close scrutiny of its eyes was unnerving – Cameron could hear the tiny grinding sounds they made as they shifted about in their marble sockets. "You look like a man cub to me. Perhaps I should eat you anyway, and be done."

"I'm her grandson," Cameron said forcefully. "Her only living relative. That means the token rightfully passes to me. You've got to respect that!"

The lion's paw lifted and Cameron instinctively ducked, but it was reaching for its nose. After what felt like an eternity – in which its claws made a horrendous scraping sound – the lion straightened.

"You can board." Its attention shifted to Morgan and Eve. "I'll eat these two instead."

"Make that starters only." Morgan snaked a hand down his neck, snagging a leather cord, and pulled up a yellowed ivory disc. "You see this? It's a bone-debt, yeah? Between Janus and my pack." He spun the disc, dangling it in front of the lion. Scratched crudely on one side was a crescent shape; the reverse had the now-familiar two-faced silhouette. "Debts have to be paid." He cast a sympathetic glance at Eve. "Sorry, no sense us both ending up lion-chow, is there?"

"Thanks *so much*," said Eve.

The lion emitted a drawn-out gravelly sound that might've been a sigh. "Yes. This is valid. It dates from the Old Time, the glory days of Rome; I can scent it. You may pass."

Morgan edged around the lion and joined Cameron in the doorway of the train.

"What about Eve?" Cameron hissed.

"I don't know, do I?"

There was a whistle scream, a *shush* of steam, and the engine began to send up fresh clouds of smoke.

"Two aboard, and the train's about to go. That leaves you." The lion eyed Eve. "Barely a snack."

"So why bother?" Eve's chin stuck out, although the tremor in her voice betrayed her anxiety. "You shouldn't eat between meals, that's what I've heard –"

"Thanks for the advice, but I think I will. You looked the most delicious anyway." With the casual grace of a predator, the lion began to amble towards her.

"Do something!" Cameron shouted.

"Like what, exactly?" Morgan shrugged wildly. "I don't want her to get munched any more than you, but right now I'm out of plans!"

"We've got to try!" Cameron dashed toward the

cat, charging at its flank, trying to shove it off course. Smashing into its stone bulk felt exactly like running into a wall. The creature didn't shift at all.

"Mmm, satisfying," said the lion. "Perhaps your friend could scritch my other side, even me out?" Another whistle-blast sounded and, with a groan of metal, the steam engine began to pull out from the station.

Eve was backing away as fast as she could. Her feet skittered on a patch of drool-marbles, and for a moment she seemed to moonwalk, then she toppled backwards onto the platform. The lion was almost on top of her.

Cameron's eyes widened. An image had shot into his head, of a vast wardrobe his dad once moved. It had seemed unshiftable, wedged into the corner of a room, but his dad had tipped the wardrobe back on one edge and handed Cameron some ball-bearings to slide underneath. Once in place, they'd been able to *roll* it...

"With me! Morgan!"

He raced to the creature's rear as the wolf-boy joined him. "When I say 'now', shove as hard as you can!"

"Wha–?"

"Don't argue – just push!" Cameron shouted. "Eve – you've gotta roll *fast*, away from the platform's edge!"

Tucking her arms in, the girl spun towards the station.

"*NOW!*"

58

Cameron and Morgan slammed their full weight into the creature's rump.

With a crunching sound the huge beast slid, its flat stone feet rolling helplessly on its own patch of marble drool. Its blank eyes bulged as it slipped and skittered. Gaining pace, it trundled forward, crashing headfirst off the platform and onto the tracks with an almighty yowl.

"That – was – amazing!" Eve gasped. "You're a genius!"

"Never mind that, come on!" Morgan gestured towards the engine that was now gathering speed, pulling away from the platform. "We've got a train to catch!"

CHAPTER 4

ROMAN RAILWAY

They leapt aboard just as the train passed the far end
of the platform, and collapsed into the carriage in a
heap. Cameron struggled to his feet, took hold of a
convenient railing, and leaned out into the rushing air
to slam the door.

"Still glad you came?"

"Definitely." Eve gave a small smile. "I've decided
it's invigorating, almost being eaten alive."

"I'll remember you said that."

The inside of the carriage was unlike any Cameron
had ever seen before. There were no rows of seats.
Instead, the space had been decked out to look like the
garden of a Mediterranean villa. Corinthian pillars
stretched from mosaic floor to ceiling, marking out
a courtyard that contained a pond and low marble
benches. Grapevines straggled round the windows,

beyond which the strange Human/Daemon mash-up of the Parallel rolled by with increasing speed. The air smelled of dry earth and honey.

A hard, abrasive sensation prompted Cameron to look down. A white kitten was winding its way round his legs. He touched its head, and found it was cold.

It stared up with empty eyes, and *miaowed* lustily.

"Great. Another stone moggie." Morgan bared his teeth. "Go away!"

"Pay no attention," a voice said airily. "He's on the mooch for peacock hearts again. He's had plenty, the beastly little horror."

"Although, what is it they say?" a second voice added in ominous tones. "A raw heart a day – keeps the physician away?"

"Oh shush. Stop trying to scare our guests," continued the first. "They've had enough of an ordeal, poor dears, getting past that self-important guardian."

"And yet that shall be as nothing," said the sinister voice, "compared to the trials that are to come."

A tapestry curtain parted. Standing in the doorway to the next carriage was a tall, muscular man dressed in a flowing toga. Curled dark hair framed broad shoulders and a most peculiar head: one set of eyes, nose and mouth pointed left, and a second, equally distinguished set of features pointed in the opposite direction.

"You've got two faces," said Eve. She clapped a hand to her mouth.

Morgan raised an eyebrow. "*Really?*"

"Well, I didn't know, did I?" she hissed. "I thought the image on the ward was symbolic..."

"Yes, dear," said the face on the left, not unkindly. "We do. It goes with the job –"

"With the Godhood of Portals, more accurately," said the face on the right. "We see everything that comes and goes –"

"All life's little entrances and exits!"

"For I look wearily to the past," right sighed, "and am filled with regret."

"Whereas I look to the future," said left, "and am delighted by possibility."

There was a blur and Janus's head spun: the curly hair somehow remaining static while the dual faces exchanged sides.

"Or is it," said the face now on the left, "that I look to the past, with fond remembrance?"

"And I look to the future, with apprehension and terror?" said right. "We're not going to tell! Believe me, darlings, we've tried prophecy. It doesn't end well."

"He's like a double act," Cameron muttered out the corner of his mouth, "but in one body."

Morgan gave his head a tiny shake. "He's no joker."

The stone kitten mewed delightedly and ran over to Janus, who dug in a pouch hanging from his toga and produced a black, withered-looking object that he threw to the ground. The kitten seized it and slunk away under the benches.

"Monster!" said both faces together, with great affection. Their blue eyes turned back to the visitors.

62

"And who has come to call on us today? Romulus and Remus, surely?"

Cameron looked blank and Morgan shrugged.

"Two wolf-boys at any rate, if my four eyes do not deceive. Whatever can they want with little old me?" Janus gestured to the marble benches, then turned to an alcove containing an amphora and some carved goblets. "You will join me in a libation?"

"Am I just invisible or something?" Eve, who'd been looking increasingly irritable, coughed loudly. "Or is this another boys' club I don't get to join?"

Janus's back stiffened. The lights flickered, and for a moment the *lackata-lackata* sound of the train's progress seemed to falter. The stone kitten yowled and darted to the far end of the carriage.

"Ah yes. The girl whose brain and body are different ages... even if her mind is fast catching up," the first voice mused. The second continued in harsher tones, "She should take care her mouth doesn't run away with her. We could so easily *show her the door*."

One of the carriage windows faded, the glass being replaced by plain wooden boards and a dented brass handle. Its outline narrowed then stretched downwards until it reached the floor. The newly formed door creaked ajar, letting in cold damp-smelling air.

"An exit." Janus poured dark red liquid into the goblets. "If you want."

"Eve, be careful," Cameron urged. He eyed the doorway, wondering which sinister daemonic dimension

63

it might lead to. "Don't annoy the, um, God. You don't know what he can do..."

"I can fight my own battles, thank you." She marched up to the tall figure in the toga and inclined her head. "Forgive me, Janus. I didn't mean to be impatient –"

"But you are impatient, aren't you?" The train shook as the wheels skipped another beat on the tracks. "Your friends carry the symbols of my wardship and my debt – they have rights. What about you?"

"Me? I'm just along for the ride... No, that's not correct. I'm..." Eve's brow furrowed. "I'm here because I chose to be. Because my home is in danger too. I wanted to come."

"All journeys begin with a choice. Where you end up, what happens *en route* – that is less predictable. For you, at least." Janus turned back to the room, a thin smile starting on his left face and spreading rightwards. He handed Eve a goblet from a cloth-covered tray. "We forgive your impudence. We have a certain... sympathy for your nature." His right face continued, more gently, "It's not easy to be more than one thing at once, is it? But it's more common than you might think."

The atmosphere in the room seemed to clear as Janus put the tray down on the bench, and handed out two further goblets. Morgan sniffed at his dubiously.

Cameron, who'd learned to be cautious accepting food and drink on the Parallel, waited a discrete interval before setting his down. "Janus, you seem to know exactly why we're here –"

"Past. Future. Insight." Janus waved a hand. "What part of that don't you understand?"

"So I'm going to get straight to the point," said Cameron. "Will you help?"

"Replace the ward? No." Janus leaned forward and whipped the cloth from the tray. A stone dagger nestled on a satin cushion. "Not unless you pay."

"Pay how?" said Cameron, acutely aware all eyes in the carriage were now fixed on the knife.

"Well... what do you think such powerful magic would be worth?" Janus ran his finger along the blade, while the tongue in his left mouth described an equally languid route along his teeth. His right face gave Cameron a direct look. "Come now... I am a Roman God after all. You can't ask for help without a sacrifice."

Cameron's mouth twitched in disgust. "Me and Morgan – and Eve too – we're good at finding things. Anything you want from the Human World or the Parallel, we're the guys who could get it. But not that. I'd never hurt anyone." He stood up and beckoned to his friends. "We shouldn't have come."

"Pity," said Janus. "Your grandmother came better prepared."

Cameron closed his eyes. "I'm not her."

"You lack her courage."

"He really doesn't," said Morgan, moving to stand by Cameron's side. "He's just not barking mad."

"Where does the train stop?" Eve added brightly. "I think we should be going."

For a long moment there was only the clack of wheels on rails, then Janus clapped his hands and laughed. "But my dears! The journey isn't over! There's still the matter of my debt to the wolves. I *insist* upon clearing it."

Morgan hesitated, but Cameron nodded. "Go on. What've we got to lose?"

The larger boy dug out the bone medallion and handed it over.

"A long time since I gave this away! Granted to the Were-brothers who founded Ancient Rome, in exchange for Temple rights. No wonder I saw them in you." Janus studied the disc, lost in remembrance. "Someone values you highly, wolf-boy, to entrust you with this."

Cameron frowned, wondering how Morgan had managed to scavenge it from the pack, but Morgan just scratched his hair.

"What can I say? I'm lovable."

"You will both follow me to the inner sanctum." Janus held one hand aloft and processed in stately strides towards the doorway that led to the next carriage. "Eve may rest here and enjoy the delights of the garden. I grant her full use of it." His second, snarkier voice filtered back through the tapestry curtain. *"Don't feed the cat!"*

As the curtain fluttered closed, Eve let out a long breath. "Well... he was very predictable and reassuring, wasn't he?"

"I revise my earlier description," said Cameron. "He must be God of Mood Swings as well."

"Not so loud, he might hear you." She shot a glance at the tapestry, then turned her attention to the panelled doorway Janus had conjured up. "I wonder where he was going to banish me?"

"Thrown to the marble lions, I expect." Morgan gave a mirthless grin. "You ok, kid?"

"Fine. You two better go, before he changes his mind."

The junction between the carriages was open, exposed to the air. Cameron gingerly stepped over the swaying gangway. The room beyond was dim, lit by candles in ornate holders. The roof vanished into the distance, and the space seemed larger than could possibly fit inside a railway carriage. As his eyes adjusted to the gloom, he saw the faint outlines of doors floating in the murky atmosphere – doors of every imaginable shape, size and description.

"What is this place?" he said, watching the drifting shapes.

"The Temple of the Door, of course." Janus threw himself onto a golden couch. "Or a portable version of it at least. The original is long lost."

"It's huge!"

"I borrow the space from human hallways. They're another part of my domain: all those doors, you see. No one ever seems to notice, even when they start tripping over shoes and umbrellas..." One Janus face gave a self-satisfied grin. The other looked exasperated, and said, "To business. Though I won't grant the ward, if you cancel my debt, I can give you something much more useful."

Morgan folded his arms. "Ward's pretty useful. What's better?"

In answer, Janus reached up, his hand cupped above his head. From every corner of the chamber the floating door outlines rushed and jostled towards him, clustering to touch his outstretched fingers. Suddenly he snatched, as if catching a moth, and the doors vanished into smoke. "I offer you this." He lowered his fist and opened it, revealing something small and shiny on his palm.

"A key," said Cameron. "An ordinary house key..."

"No. It's *every* key, distilled from the essence of every door. The Omniclavis! There isn't a lock it won't open, not anywhere in the worlds." Janus held out his hands, the Omniclavis in one, the bone debt in the other. "Well, what's it to be?"

Morgan's eyes shone green. "I reckon we take it. More use than a mouldy old bone..."

"Then the deal is done!" Janus cried before Cameron could speak, his fist clenching tight around the bone debt. Yellow dust ran through his fingers to the ground. He flung the key in Morgan's direction, and stretched like a cat. "My debt is cleared. Now pay attention, wolf-boys: three times only the Omniclavis will work – and then it returns to me."

"Hold on. You didn't mention that!" said Cameron.

"No?" Janus lay back on the couch, affecting a look of innocence. "Must've slipped my mind."

"That bone-thing was our bargaining tool." Cameron turned to Morgan. "I hope you know what you're doing."

"Reckon so. We've still got Grey, Black and their summons to deal with. Bet we can steal a march on them with this."

"Oh, don't bicker. This was meant to be." Four eyes fixed Cameron with an ironic gaze. "It *augurs* well for your future."

Cameron opened his mouth to ask the Roman God what he meant, but at that same moment an enormous shuddering *thunk* shook the carriage. The room swayed giddily from left to right as if the train was dancing on the rails. "What happened?"

Janus said nothing, but closed his eyes and started to hum a little tune.

There was metallic rending sound, like something being ripped open, and a cry rang out. Morgan's head jerked in the direction of the other carriage. "That's Eve! Come on!"

They darted for the gangway.

In the garden room, two huge blundering grey shapes were stumbling to their feet. Each resembled an over-inflated puffball parody of a man: the body and limbs bloated and swollen.

"They came through the roof! They just tore it open!" Eve ducked as one blob swung an arm at her. It missed, and connected wetly with a column. There was a strange, sickly sweet smell as it drew its arm back, and Cameron saw part of the stonework had vanished, leaving behind a gap as if it had been eaten away.

"Eve, get out!" he yelled.

"Oh thanks! I'd never have thought of that."

She leapt over the marble benches, and darted round the pond to the other side of the carriage. Remorselessly, the blob men followed.

The stone kitten hissed, driven from its hiding place, and raced past Cameron to the gangway.

"I'm gonna get Janus. He's got the power to stop this –" Morgan loped in the direction of the Temple of the Door. "Try and hold them off!" he called over his shoulder.

"With what, exactly?" Cameron seized a heavy amphora and flung it at the nearest blob. It squelched into the creature's back, which puffed and absorbed the jug whole. The grey skin bubbled and flattened, and the creature seemed to grow...

Fragments of Morgan's shouted conversation with the God of Doors echoed back along the gangway:

"Why won't you help?"

"It's not what I do."

"What d'you mean – it's not your *style*?"

"No, it's not *what I do*. Past and future, remember?"

Eve was edging along the wall as the blob-creatures lumbered ever closer. Her back touched the wooden doorway Janus had summoned up. She seized the handle. "I'm gonna risk it, there's no other way –"

"Eve, no! You don't know where it goes!"

She yanked the door open. An expression of surprise ran over her face. "Cameron, it's –

The blobs threw themselves forward. Eve stepped through, slamming the door behind her. It vanished

70

instantly. With an aggrieved roar, the blobs turned to Cameron.

Cameron's eyes widened. *Their faces resembled a crudely formed version of Mr Grey's...*

He backed away down the carriage, pushing through the tapestry that covered the link to the Temple of the Door.

Morgan was in the doorway of the next carriage, waving frantically. "Jump across!" he shouted. "That stone moggy's only gone and pulled out the pin that holds –"

There was a sharp, scraping sound and suddenly Morgan was a lot further away.

The distance between the carriages was growing

The gangway plank had gone – fallen away onto the track. Morgan's temple carriage – still coupled to the driving steam engine – was fast gaining speed, getting further and further ahead. Cameron's garden carriage meanwhile continued to travel at an incredible pace, carried forward by momentum alone. The wind whipped in his face, roaring in his ears like a howl...

"Jump!" yelled Morgan across the void.

"I can't!" Cameron screamed back as the rails raced below. "It's going too fast! I'll fall under –"

"You've got to!"

Cameron turned back to the carriage – the grey blob men were almost upon him, their lumpen features contorted into angry leers.

He took a deep breath. There wasn't anything else he could do –

He jumped.

CHAPTER 5

ABRUPTLY HUMAN

"Yeeaaaaaaa–
ooooooooooow!"

In midair, Cameron's shout turned from a human cry of terror to something else entirely. The carriage in front was too far away, so he leapt at an angle, heading for the railway sidings instead. A steep bank covered with a tangle of grass, trees and bushes rushed towards him.

No clear place to fall.

This is gonna hurt.

His vision sharpened – like autofocus on a camera kicking in – and everything seemed to slow.

He would bend his legs and land on all fours, duck and roll –

An impact – hard earth, stones – a tumble – the world turned 360 degrees. The air was knocked out of him.

72

Cameron hit the ground in the shape of a wolf.

He had no time to take stock of his unexpected transformation. He bounded up, wolf claws fast finding purchase, and shook free the fragments of human clothing that still clung to his newly furred body. A sharp pain stabbed in his front shoulder. He ignored it, and zigzagged sure-footedly down the bank.

The pace of the engine-less carriage was only just beginning to falter. He darted past its side – running along the edge of the tracks – then back onto the line in front.

Cameron could call on a good turn of speed in wolf-form, but he was no match for Janus's locomotive at full throttle. The front carriage continued to gain distance. He could see two grey men swarming up the end of the coach and onto the roof, pulling themselves forward, hand over puffy hand. They must've jumped the gap just after he leapt from the train.

They weren't after him... Whatever they wanted was still onboard.

With a whistle-scream, the train snaked into a tunnel and Cameron followed. The light level fell away and his eyes narrowed instinctively. In the confined space, the steam from the engine billowed into a thick cloud. Only the greasy touch of the railway sleepers below his pads let him know he wasn't drifting away into muggy darkness. Scent drew him on: the steam mingled with the sugary-sweet mushroom stink of the Greys.

Cameron's lip curled, exposing his incisors. There

was something subtly wrong about the Greys. They provoked him – and not just by threatening his friends. It was like they didn't belong, like they had no right to be on the Parallel.

Like it was his duty to chase them down...

Daylight flared, and he was once again outside. The track banked sharply round a double bend, heading towards a second tunnel. Set into a high wall beneath the city streets, the entrance was low, with jagged flagstones projecting down like teeth. The opening burned with a rippling red light.

Cameron slowed. The Parallel song sounded a warning inside his mind: this tunnel wasn't just another part of the Parallel landscape, but a portal leading on to the Daemon World itself...

The train hared into it and vanished, swallowed up by the stony maw.

A tearing sensation ran through his chest. His wolf-self desperately wanted to follow – to throw himself in and to hell with the consequences. But his human side urged caution. Morgan had warned him about Daemonic, told him most of the inhabitants hadn't encountered a living human being in centuries. Even in wolf form, Cameron would be in danger...

Morgan.

His best friend.

Who he couldn't leave to fight the Greys alone...

Head down, Cameron raced forward, only for the decision to be snatched away from him. With a guttural sound, the yawning tunnel mouth flexed and contracted. The flagstones bit down, clamping into the earth and sealing the entrance shut. Cameron skidded to a halt.

A dirt-flecked lightbulb pinged, calmly illuminating a sign:

PARALLEL LINE INTERCHANGE
* Daemon World Transfer in Progress *
Access to authorised vehicles only
by Order of Janus

He reared up and howled. As he beat out his frustration on the stonework, his paws resolved into fists, and he found himself abruptly human once more.

One of the many difficult things about being a werewolf was sorting out the clothes. He'd said that to Eve once, and she'd almost died laughing.

"You've problems matching your t-shirt to your pointy ears and tail?"

That hadn't been what he'd meant at all, *clearly*. He'd been talking about practicalities: the sort of things Morgan – who had a lifetime of Were experience – guided him on. You had to be ready to take on a distinctly different body shape for three Fat Moon nights a month. You needed clothes that would slip off easily when the change took over, and a stash for when you shifted back the next day. You needed food: plenty of it, both before and after, to fuel the complex process that re-knitted and reshaped bones and cartilage, and grew fur, teeth and claws.

If you didn't prepare – as Cameron had explained to Eve – the consequences could be anything from hugely dangerous (turning into a large and extremely *hungry* predator) to a little embarrassing (transforming back into a naked human).

"So if you ever meet a big black wolf looking sheepish one morning –"

"I should search out a sweatshirt and some joggers, turn my back, and not ask any awkward questions?"

"That's about right, yeah."

He'd had no warning this time, Cameron reflected, as he tracked his way back along the rails, shivering. He would gladly have turned wolf again, donning his snug fur against the cold, but he didn't know how. The wolf lay buried deep inside him most of the time, and he had no way to reach it.

Morgan had told him that down in the Daemon World, Weres could shapeshift whenever they chose. On the Parallel and in the Human World, however, the full moon would call you each month, triggering the change whether you wanted it or not. Full-blooded Weres could – with proper training – resist the call, or at least lessen its effects, but even they could not summon it at will. And as for changing into a wolf outwith the nights of the Fat Moon? That was completely unheard of.

76

Twice now, the shift had happened of its own volition. First fighting off the Weaver Daemon, and again when he'd leapt from the train. He'd been frightened the first time, uncertain what was happening, but on this occasion his overwhelming emotion was one of relief. The wolf's agility had allowed him to walk away from that jump with no worse injury than a staved shoulder. Would a human have survived? It seemed to Cameron the change had come exactly when he'd needed it most.

The wolf had saved him, and he was grateful.

Scanning the tracks around the point he'd jumped, he managed to find both his trainers and pulled them on. His jeans and jacket had fallen a little further away, and proved to be in worse condition: ripped apart as he'd transformed. He felt in his pockets to retrieve his keys and belongings, and drew out a silver packet: a foil blanket, like marathon runners wore, all neatly folded up. It was leftover from a trade with a wood spirit who'd exchanged knowledge of herbs for frost protection for her saplings. Shaking the blanket open, Cameron draped it over his shoulders and wrapped it tight around his body.

He'd pass for human now – at least for one daft enough to go running in January – and not draw many suspicious glances on his way back to the shop. He'd organised with Eve and Morgan to meet there if they ever got separated.

Shifting to the Human World, he walked along the cycle path, nodding to the occasional fellow runner. As he climbed the stairs that led up to Scotland Street in Edinburgh's New Town, he spotted a semi-circular opening recessed into the wall. A well-used basketball hoop was attached to a row of steel bars blocking off the dank space beyond.

He'd found the Human World equivalent of the tunnel to Daemonic. Just another forgotten part of the city. People probably never even gave it as second glance as they ran or cycled past, or shot baskets at the shuttered gate.

He hesitated, feeling a surge of anger. If Morgan and Eve hadn't made it out, he'd come back here and tear those bars down. *He'd force his way in, find a way back to them somehow...*

His hands shook.

Perhaps the wolf wasn't buried so deeply after all.

"Morgan? Eve?"

Cameron's voice echoed back from the deserted shop. It had been a vain hope they'd both be waiting, full of stories about their adventures.

Still, it wasn't as if he was without resources... He'd learnt so much running the business this past year. There were people and daemons he could talk to, books he could consult. All sorts of things! He'd track down Morgan and Eve, rescue them if he had to, respond to the Court summons, take on Mr Grey and Dr Black...

He sank into the chair, momentarily overwhelmed. Where to begin?

On the corner of the desk, the lump that had been Mr Grey's chin squatted. It seemed bigger than he remembered, and he couldn't shake the uncanny notion it was watching him. *What connection did it have to the Greys on the train?* He prodded it with a pencil and it pulsed damply.

He moved to the storeroom, returning with a fresh set of clothes and a covered plate. He scoffed the stale cake from below the cover, recharging some vital energy, but his real goal was the lid. With a swift motion, he clapped the patterned dome down over the lump.

"That'll teach you to sit and look at me with... no eyes."

A message light blinked from the answerphone and he eagerly thumbed a button, hoping for news. It triggered a long series of clicks.

"– Cam! It's Amy! Have you *still* not got a new mobile? Seriously? Who doesn't have a mobile? Well, you don't obviously; otherwise I wouldn't be leaving you this message... Anyway, I had to let you know, she got it! My old mum's gone and got the job! So we're gonna be moving through to Edinburgh. Can you believe it? Not right away – I'm gonna have to stay with my nan till term's over, but this summer – boom! This town isn't going to know what hit it! And we can go to the same school again –"

There was a garbled sound and the message juddered to a halt. He opened the lid of the machine and a cassette ejected, spewing yards of tape. Like nearly everything else in the shop, the answerphone was years out of date.

"Oh Amy. You broke the phone. You talked it to death."

They'd been friends for ages, growing up in Cauldlockheart, back when life was simple and he'd lived with his dad. Cameron had been awkward and uninterested in sport, preferring daydreams about guitars and bands; Amy big and bolshy, with a lilting Scots-Italian accent and a refusal to back down in a fight. Seeing less of her was the one thing he regretted about leaving that gloomy town.

He began the laborious process of detangling the tape. Somehow, that felt easier to deal with than his real problems...

He'd never found a way to explain his new life to Amy. No matter how great she was, she was still only human – and human without Inheritance at that. She had no idea the Parallel even existed. One of the most terrifying moments he'd had was coming back from a trading mission to find her unexpectedly in the shop, deep in conversation with Eve.

"We've been discussing your faults," Eve said brightly. "Which are numerous."

"What are you doing here? How did you even find this place?"

"Weird and arcane powers!" Amy flared her eyes and made witchy movements with her hands. "Also known as Google. I put in 'record shop', 'Edinburgh' and 'scary old woman' and there was a surprisingly long page. Loads of people going on about stuff they'd found here, and some pretty bizarre rumours too... Eve's told me everything."

"She has?" Cameron shot an alarmed look at Eve.

"Isn't it strange?" Eve said pointedly. "How before your dad died, neither of us knew *we had a cousin?*"

"Oh! Yes. That was... odd."

"I could tell you were related at once, as soon as I looked at her," Amy said, oblivious. "Eve must be *way* more fun to live with than your gran. When's the old lady getting back from her research trip anyway?"

Amy was relatively contained during term time – she never had much money for the train – but if she lived in the same city... How long would it be till she found out all about him?

Cameron sometimes felt like he was two people: the ordinary boy from Cauldlockheart, a bit shy and lacking in confidence, and the world-shifting wolf-boy who had a totally mad and often wonderful existence. He loved his new life, and fiercely wanted to protect it. Now it seemed like his identities were colliding – just as things were falling apart.

He picked up one of the guitars he kept at the shop, placed it on his lap and began to absent-mindedly pick out a tune. Music had always helped him, at both the happiest and saddest times in his life. It was something he could focus on, and lose himself in: a perfect world of its own, far from any worries or anxiety.

He was just contemplating a particularly tricky chord progression when a movement out the corner of his eye distracted him. The cake cover was shuffling along the desk... The dome bumped into the discarded cassette, lifted, drew in the tape, and moved on.

He put the guitar down, and moved quietly to the desk. He whipped the lid off. A long brown strand of tape was vanishing into the lump, sucked in like spaghetti. It froze, mid-sook.

"Caught you! What are you up to?"

A tiny mouth puckered, revealing chalky grey teeth. "You are ordered to attend the Court of the Parallel. The case of Dr Black versus Lady Ives o' the Black Hill is called!"

He stared at the lump. "That wasn't meant to be for another two days!"

"The case has been brought forward," it gurgled smugly. "You must attend. You must produce Isobel Ives or surrender your tenancy of the shop."

"You can't do that!" Cameron thought frantically. They had gone off in search of the ward so they'd have a safe base of operations – not that it had worked out. Morgan and Eve were still missing, and he hadn't even *begun* to tackle the threat posed by Black and Grey. "What if I say no? You can't make me."

"Then action will be taken." The lump rolled along the desk, its grey dough flesh squashing into and over the answermachine. There was a suckering sound, and the machine vanished. The lump grew bigger.

"All problems will be *absorbed*..."

CHAPTER 6

GUIDED BY LAMPS

A fancy bookcase swung aside to reveal the top of a flight of stairs. A lantern, hanging by a metal ring from a staff, lay propped at an angle against the wall.

Cameron peered down the stairwell, which spiralled away into darkness. "This way to the Court," he said to himself. He reached for the lantern.

"You are expected. You will follow me."

The staff lifted itself from the ground and swung forward, as if being used as a walking stick by some unseen person. The metal tip made a *pock! pock!* sound as it descended the wooden steps.

"Portable lighting. That's original." The pool of light was moving fast and Cameron hurried after. "Hey, wait for me! It's pretty dark."

"Then let the light of justice be your guide." The

flame flickered, its voice a hollow whisper. "That was by means of a joke... You didn't find it funny."

Cameron drew in air through his teeth. "Not really. I've got a lot on my mind."

"I try to lighten the mood if I can. So many people never leave the Court. We may as well make their stay as pleasant as possible."

"That fills me with confidence," said Cameron. The stairs creaked beneath his feet. "Is it far to go?"

"Quite a distance. Nearly all the way down," said the lantern. "The Court was set up to deal with cases that uniquely concern the Parallel. It was felt it should be located between both worlds. You will have passed the Human law chambers on your way in?"

Cameron nodded.

Grey's double chin had provided directions. The lump had become increasingly strident, its warnings accompanied by a series of bleeps, gargles and clicks from its innards. "A non-appearance at Court is as good as an admission of guilt. You may be judged in your absence –"

"Oh belt up." Cameron had popped the plate-cover back on, ignoring the indignant cries. The lump was sounding increasingly like the pompous daemon that had spawned it. "Don't think you're going squelching about free-range while I'm out either." He added some strips of parcel tape, strapping the cover in place.

He had dashed about the shop, looking for anything he could find that might show his connection to

Grandma Ives, and so to the trading business he'd taken over after she'd vanished. Given that he couldn't whistle-up the old lady in the flesh, perhaps he could prove to the Court he was her rightful successor.

That strategy hadn't worked with Janus, but it was the best he could come up with.

Gathering together his papers and documents, he had scribbled a quick and only slightly desperate-sounding note to Eve and Morgan. He left the shop, climbed the hill to the oldest part of the city, and headed for a huddle of buildings off Parliament Square, set back from the Royal Mile. Tagging onto a procession of dark-suited lawyers and their clients, Cameron had slipped in.

A series of elegant rooms reminded him of the costume dramas Eve sometimes watched on telly (the sort that usually made him long for an invasion by killer robots). On entering a grand multi-tiered library, he shifted through to the Parallel. The bookcase alcove opened up, as if it had been waiting for him.

The air was turning stuffy as he descended, the spiral stair passing balcony after balcony. Below, he could see the blurred outlines of lights bobbing through the gloom. Daemons of all kinds followed in their wake: antlered Cervidae, their heads bowed; impossibly glamorous Fey; whisker-faced Selkies, Moss Mites, Tree Spirits, Red Caps…

"Lanterns," he said, as his eyes adjusted. "They're all lanterns – moving by themselves, leading people through the dark."

"Weir lamps, to be accurate."

"There's a difference?"

"Ah ha." The light flared. "We *are* lanterns, yes. But we're Weir lamps too. Named after the mad Major. You'll know of Major Weir?"

Cameron shook his head.

"He was infamous in his day, as was his walking stick, which he'd send out on errands across the city."

Cameron thought he'd have remembered seeing a flock of unaccompanied lights-on-sticks marching about the place. "When was this?"

"Oh... 1670 or so."

"I'm *fifteen*."

"Are you? The major's long gone, I suppose, but his stick – and its scions – are condemned to walk on." The lamplight dimmed and turned a rusty orange. "And so, that is what we do. Until our task is done."

The staff tilted back to block Cameron as a procession of monks in purple robes joined the stair. They were chanting and carrying aloft a banner strung between uplifted poles.

"The Joyful People of the Banner," the lantern whispered.

"They don't look very happy to me," said Cameron, noting the monks' downcast faces and mournful song.

"They're in thrall to the Weaver Queen," said the lamp. "The joy is all hers. I don't believe their happiness enters into the arrangement."

As the banner flowed past, the red eyes of the largest Weaver Daemon Cameron had ever seen glared back – and he swiftly became very interested in the banister.

"So not a fan," he muttered. "I don't know how they stand it."

"We all have to serve, in our way." The lamp resumed their descent. "And who will be representing your case at Court?"

"No one." Cameron gave a tiny shrug. "There's just me."

There was a sound like wind blowing on a candle and the light guttered. "That is not a wise choice."

"It wasn't a choice at all, trust me. There was no time."

"We're about to pass the advocates' boxes. You could still seek counsel?"

The lantern slowed as the spiral stair touched the next balcony. It led Cameron past a line of wooden crates that reminded him uncomfortably of coffins. A stained and yellowed barrister wig rested at the head of each.

As he watched, a couple of forest daemons tentatively approached a box, and posted a scroll through a letterbox on top. There was a pause and a puff of smoke rose up from the slot. The wig lifted as the smoke beneath billowed out into a tall thin shape.

"They're in luck," said the lamp. "The advocate has agreed to take their case."

The silhouette solidified into a gaunt-faced man with swept-back hair. He shook out a heavy cloak that hung from his shoulders like wings.

"Correct me if I'm wrong," said Cameron, as the pale man adjusted his wig using surprisingly sharp fingernails, "but when you say 'advocate', you mean *vampire*, right?"

"Vampires are suited to law. They have a long life, good memory, and are content to study for decades in darkened rooms," said the lamp. "On the other hand, they do tend to bleed their clients dry."

Cameron managed a mirthless laugh.

"It was not intended as a joke, sir. Many of our best legal minds belong to that clan, and prefer to take their payment in blood."

The advocate raised his arms, enveloped one of the furry daemons in the folds of his cloak, and lowered his head. Cameron shivered and turned away. "I think I'll defend myself. I've got enough problems without adding a vampire to my case."

"Then we shall proceed. We are nearly there."

The balcony became narrower. Eventually the boards diverged, splitting into two paths that ran in both directions around a circular opening, about half the size of a football pitch. At regular intervals around its circumference, burly bull daemons stood to attention beside gleaming metal winches. The Weir lamp came to rest by the balustrade, and Cameron peered over.

The wooden panelling of the Court walls gave way to densely packed brick, and then in turn to bare rock. A warm sulphurous wind blew in his face. From somewhere deep below, a distant red light rippled and pulsed, reminding him of the tunnel that led to Daemonic.

He couldn't see the bottom at all.

Cameron cleared his throat. Heights had never been his favourite thing. "That's the Court?"

"As I said, it lies between the worlds."

"There's nothing down there – just a drop!"

"There will be. The jury is going in now."

On the left-hand side of the pit, a line of daemons and humans were being guided down steps onto a suspended platform, not unlike the sort used by window-cleaners to access the sides of very tall buildings. Working as a team, four bull daemons began to turn the winches at either end. Sweat rose from their swarthy flesh and jets of steam pumped from their nostrils as the platform was lowered, and the jury vanished from sight.

"You're completely out of your depth, you know." Leather shoes clicked on boards, and Cameron turned to see Dr Black. He gave a smug smile and brushed dust from his lapels. "You've no idea what you've got yourself into, have you, boy?"

Cameron's brow furrowed. The humans he'd met on the Parallel had been eccentrics or scholars; adventurers, visionaries or mad men. Even his gran, who had prided herself on her respectable appearance, had revealed a knife-sharp inner core. It was as if the Parallel Inheritance – that strange power that burned inside them – always found a way to creep to the surface. They were all outsiders – and Cameron counted himself in that category – different in some way, by fate or by choice.

Dr Black, by contrast, didn't seem to match the Parallel 'type'. All the things that would make him seem unremarkable on the city streets – his suit, his clippered hair, his neatness and blandly handsome features – made him stand out in the murky subterranean court. He was just too normal.

Why was he here?

What was he up to?

Cameron took a tighter hold on the folder he'd carried from the shop: the proof of his Parallel heritage. "Out my depth? I don't reckon so. I've looked things in the face you wouldn't believe. I've survived time-eating bats, Gods of Doorways, Gods of Winter, Mrs Ferguson... even my gran." He shrugged. "You though... you must've snuck in with a crash course: *Daemon Parallel for Dummies*."

Black's mouth contorted, and for a second Cameron thought he was going to hit him. "What do you know about the things I've been through – the things I've found –"

A blubbery hand clamped onto Dr Black's shoulder. "Not another word, Dr Black! Most unprofessional! We shall settle this matter in Court, properly, like GentleDaemons." Mr Grey stepped from the shadows. He was dressed in the garb of an advocate, with a black robe and a coarse horsehair wig perched on his greasy head.

"Properly? That's a joke," said Cameron. "So you're

not going to hijack this too, like you did Janus's train?"

"He can't know about the engine –" Black began, but Grey's hand squeezed tighter and the anger seemed to drain from his colleague's face.

Grey's sugary-mushroom stink washed towards Cameron.

"You will discover, young sir, that in Court there is such a thing as 'burden of proof'. And you have no proof – no proof at all."

Leading the now docile Black, Grey retreated to the other side of the pit. He lumbered into a pulpit-type box, his swollen body just squeezing in, while Black stepped into a cradle of rope that drew closed around him. The bull daemons began to heave and strain and soon Grey and Black were both lowered over the edge and into the pit.

"You must go now as well." The lamp indicated a further cradle. "In the absence of a proper defence counsel, I will accompany you, if you like, and try to shed a little light on proceedings?" It flared brightly as a bull daemon unhooked it from the top of the walking stick, and threaded its metal ring onto a rope.

"That'd be good. I think I'm gonna need all the help I can get." Cameron watched as the rope lattice tightened above his head. He took a firm grip of the sides. The cradle twirled sickeningly, spinning from left to right. "How come Grey and the jury get boxes to travel in, and I'm stuck in this fishing net?"

"Historical tradition. Both you and your opponent must enter the Court this way." The lamp glowed orange-green. "In times gone by, the loser of the case would have their cords cut, and so would fall below."

Cameron's feet paddled awkwardly as the rope mesh shifted. He tried not to look through to the empty air beneath. "How historic is historic, exactly? Very, very long ago?"

"Would it help you to know?"

He shut his eyes. "Maybe not."

Winched by the sweating bull daemons, the cradle swung over the edge of the pit and began its juddering path down.

CHAPTER 7

THE COURT OF
THE PARALLEL

Grey began by producing the will he'd wielded in
the shop. A winged gargoyle flew the document over
to Cameron, who stared at it, unable to decipher its
meaning.

More Latin. He bit his lip. If Eve was here, she
could've translated. *Where had she got to?*

Grey launched into a list of case histories that he
said were similar to the one he was presenting to the
court – none of which meant anything to Cameron.
He droned on, waving bundles of papers, while his
spare hand clutched damply at his lapel. Dr Black
swung in the rope cradle next to Grey, his legs
crossed and his hands cupped in his lap. His face was
oddly blank, as though thinking of other matters
entirely.

The air in the Court shimmered with heat, and visibility across the chasm was poor. Cameron screwed up his eyes, trying to ascertain how Grey's speech was going down with the jury. Several were from daemon clans he recognised: a Cervidae with towering antlers pawed at his bench, while a Weaver glowered from a flag strung between knitting needles. He doubted he could count on either to be sympathetic.

Others were unfamiliar, their attitudes harder to predict, like the column of light that held a single floating eye, or the metal beetle with mandibles that clattered like an agitated typewriter. A couple were even human, or at least human-shaped: a twinge of his wolf-senses told him the girl in the ragged dress was Were. She looked as nonplussed as he felt by Grey's lengthy spiel. He wondered if he'd met her before, in the rundown cinema Morgan used to hang out in with the other pack teenagers...

The wolf girl caught his eye and pouted her lips in an ironic kiss.

He blushed and looked away.

"You need to pay attention," the lamp chided, "in case there's anything you object to."

"How would I even know?" Cameron hissed back. "He might as well be talking Japanese. At least then I'd recognise 'yes', 'no' and 'help, our city is being attacked by a giant lizard'."

The lamplight turned a curious green.

"Old Godzilla movies. It doesn't matter..."

"And finally," Grey held aloft another bundle, "I

would draw Your Honour's attention to the case of Helenus versus Jackson in 1897 –"

"Yes, Grey. I am fully aware of such precedent. I set much of it myself, before reaching my current exalted position," the judge rumbled, his talons clacking on the lectern.

While the jury, prosecution and defence had all been lowered into the Court, the judge had made his entrance from the opposite direction. A rush of air had set the cradles swaying as a dark shape spiralled up from below. He had circled the pit, coming to rest with a thump of leathery wings on a ledge that projected from the rock wall.

The judge seemed more bat than human: his ears were pointed and his mouth lifted up into a peak. His ancient face was bleached, the eye sockets dry and withered. White needle-sharp fangs projected from under his upper lip.

"The Lord Justice is blind," the lamp had explained. "It doesn't matter whether you're human or daemon, rich or poor, magically adept or inept. All citizens of the Parallel are equal before him."

The judge's truncated bat-nose lifted, as though sensing Cameron's wary gaze. "Well, Mr Duffy, do you have a response to Mr Grey's opening speech? Do you contest the validity of the will?"

"I don't, Your Honour."

"Then the case shall be brief!" Grey oozed. "My Lord, I move to –"

"I don't contest it," said Cameron, his voice echoing

across the chasm, "because I wouldn't know how to. I'd never even *heard* of this thing until three days ago, when these two came pushing their way into my shop. And more than that, I don't understand it. I can't read a word –"

"Outrageous! My Lord Justice, this is dissembling of the highest order!" Grey huffed. "The will is *entirely* comprehensible. It is written in a long-established and very simple *human* tongue –"

"Which I don't speak! No one does –"

"Ignorance is no defence, as I'm sure my Lord would agree –"

"ENOUGH!" The judge thumped his lectern. "You will conduct yourselves in an orderly manner! Mr Duffy, I am satisfied that Grey's account of the document is both accurate and relevant. The tenancy of the business is limited to the lifespan of the human named. Will you accept my judgement on this matter, as a Justice Lord of the Parallel?"

"Careful now," the lamp muttered, its light fluttering.

"Yes." Cameron's grip tightened on the rope-lattice around him. "I suppose I've got to."

"Very well then. Mr Grey, you may continue."

"With pleasure, my Lord Justice." Grey smirked and gestured, his sagging arm spilling from his robe. "The case that has been brought before you by my client, the learned Dr Black, is no mere quibble over tenancy. No! There are wider issues at stake – issues that concern the well-being of us all."

What's the old puffball up to now? Cameron leant forward, trying to ignore the corresponding lurch in the opposite direction from the cradle that held him.

"Three centuries ago – when the mages Mitchell and Astredo engineered their Split to separate the Daemon World from its Human twin – the humans were, for the most part, an uncomplicated folk, basic in understanding and ability." Grey paused, and affected an innocent expression. "Some might say the defence's lamentable ignorance of Latin demonstrates little has changed..."

There were a series of sniggers from the jury box, which jiggled lightly on its ropes.

"Oh come on!" said Cameron. "That was a cheap shot!"

"I'm inclined to agree," said the judge. "You will confine yourself to the facts, Mr Grey."

"I humbly *beg* the Court's forgiveness," Grey bowed his head, "but my feeble attempt at wit masks graver concerns. The humans have not remained in this primitive state, much as it might amuse us to think so..." He swivelled to address the jury. "We all understand, do we not, that every creature requires a predator?"

There were murmurs of assent. The typewriter beetle chattered, and the Weaver Daemon vibrated on its flag.

"Cut off from the, ah, *moderating* influence of Daemon World," Grey gave a sickly smile, "the humans have multiplied unchecked. Their minds have grown in sophistication and cunning. Their science has advanced at a mighty rate. They may now send images through the ether, travel at great speed, overrun and destroy their environment. Their technologies are almost indistinguishable from our magics –"

"Oy! Excuse me, but why the history lesson? What's this got to do with *anything*?" Cameron waved his hands. "We're here because of my shop – my daft little business – not all this stuff."

The judge's talons tapped. "Another fair observation, if somewhat emotionally put. Well, Mr Grey? How does this concern us?"

"I bow to Your Honour's wisdom, of course," Grey grovelled, his wobbly chin touching the top of the prosecution box, "but is the Court of the Parallel's concern not uniquely about how the worlds of Humans and Daemons clash and intersect?"

"You have my attention, Grey. For now." The Judge's talons tapped, slower still. "Do not squander it. The Court's patience is not infinite."

"My point is this, Your Honour. The humans' quest for knowledge has so far been contained. Their focus has been on their own world, and the limits of space their crude projectiles can reach. But how long will it remain so? How long before their destructive appetite looks inward? How long before the Parallel – *before the Daemon World itself* – becomes a target for investigation and acquisition?"

"I will solve it!" In his cradle, Dr Black sat upright,

muttering furiously under his breath. "Understand the worlds, and I solve the problem. Understand the worlds, and –"

Grey's milky eyes bulged, and Black slumped.

What was that all about? Cameron wondered, but Grey was already addressing the jury again.

"The business known as 'Scott & Forceworthy's Musical Bazaar' functions as a site of inter-world trade: shifting goods between the Human and Daemon realms, via the Parallel. I would ask you, my fellow citizens, is that an enterprise we should permit? When *every daemon artefact* that reaches the human world increases our chance of detection, should this so-called 'daft little business' be allowed to continue – especially under the control of one ignorant human boy?"

The jury burst into an uproar of cheers, jeers, yells, clicks and howls. Grey's chest puffed, his sickly odour flooding the court.

"Oh, this is complete rubbish!" Cameron shouted, his agitation causing the rope cradle to swing. "What are you on about, you –"

"Order! Order in Court!" The judge's fist slammed into the lectern and the cries and mutters died down. "The defence will show respect. You will employ suitable terminology when addressing the Court."

"Objection," the lamp quietly prompted. "That's what you say..."

"Ta!" Cameron raised his voice and spoke to the pit. "Ok, I object. Objection! This is me, objecting!"

"And what is your objection?" said the judge.

"*This is rubbish* – that's my objection!"

A fresh cacophony burst out.

"Mr Duffy –" the judge warned.

"Listen! First up, my shop – it's not just me that runs it. There's Morgan and Eve too. A pure daemon and a girl who used to work for a daemon! We know about the two worlds we're dealing with – we're not just messing about –"

"And where are these people that you say are so involved?" interrupted Grey. "They don't seem to be with you in Court."

"If they aren't," said Cameron through gritted teeth, "it's not because they didn't want to be. It's because their train ran into something very large, grey and nasty."

Grey opened his mouth to protest, but Cameron pressed on.

"More than that, our business – the one Mr Grey's trying to shut down – it's helped! Helped lots of daemons. Ok, some of you can travel in the human world unnoticed, if you're a Were or a shape-shifter or whatever, but most can't. You just stand out too much! And what about those daemons – those without the Parallel Inheritance – who can't leave the Daemon World at all?"

He threw his arms wide, trying to draw the attention of all the many and varied creatures present in the Court.

"What do you do, when your magic needs a particular ingredient, or you can't get a certain book

– or you want a smartphone so you can watch humans falling over on YouTube? You turn to us. You need us! You need people like me and Morgan and Eve, who can move between the worlds for trade. You need us for all sorts of things!"

There were mutterings from the jury. Their mood was changing. At the back, a fey woman with iridescent bluebottle wings gave Cameron a discreet thumbs up. He was doing it. *He was winning them over!*

He turned back to Grey. The bloated daemon was looking cowed. "All this stuff you've been saying, trying to scare us with stories of humans and their greed, it's not..."

"...not 'relevant'," whispered the lamp.

"Yes, it's not relevant! Exactly! It's got *nothing* to do with why we're here!"

Grey's face took on an even more ashen shade than usual. "It's not? You mean... I've overlooked something?" He began to sheaf frantically through his notes. "Because I don't think I can have..."

He's on the run, Cameron thought. He swung in his cradle with a swagger. *Ha! Now to finish him off...*

"That's right! This case isn't about whether I can or should trade with daemons –"

"It isn't?" Grey's sparse eyebrows rose.

"No! It isn't even about whether the shop gets to sell old records or mouldy guitars or whatever, it's about whether Gran's still alive. *That's* all your stupid will is about. *That's* what it comes down to, that's..."

Cameron tailed off as a slow handclap ricocheted round the Court.

"I am *indebted* to the opposing counsel for crystallising the issue." Grey held his sweating palms apart. "So you agree that the case stands or falls on whether you can produce your grandmother: Lady Ives o' the Black Hill?"

"Yes, but –"

"Then I challenge you. I challenge the defence! Produce her!" Grey sneered. "Show us the lady – *or give up the shop.*"

There was a churning sensation in the pit of Cameron's stomach. He'd let himself get carried away and talked round to the very thing he'd been trying to avoid.

He knew he couldn't produce Gran. He hadn't seen her since that terrible night, high on Arthur's Seat, when she vanished into a swirling vortex. Even if she were still alive in there – even if he knew of a way to bring her out – he doubted he would go through with it. Not after all she'd done. Not after the thing she'd tried to do.

Grey turned triumphantly to face the judge. "Your Honour, the case is simple. There is no evidence that Lady Ives exists in any of the realms – Daemonic, Humanian or Parallel. I have consulted the very best sources, scryers and seers. She is not to be found. We must conclude she is deceased. The consequences are clear."

"Yes." The judge nodded. "I believe I agree. Either Ms Ives is alive and the shop is hers – or she is not, and it is forfeit." He reached for his gavel, readying to pronounce judgement.

High above, at the pit rim, a yellow light began to wink on and off.

"I'm getting a message," whispered Cameron's Weir lamp. "Someone wants to send a witness for you. They say they're a friend. Will you accept?"

"Who is it?" Cameron craned his head. "Never mind. I'll take anyone! It's not like I could be any worse off."

The lamp blinked an acknowledgement. "They're lowering her down."

"Her?" Could it be Eve – at last? What had she found?

The winches creaked and turned. As he stared up, he caught a flash of silver hair... sensible shoes... formal, old-fashioned clothes... a scent like strong coffee mixed with lavender.

"No. It couldn't be – It's not possible..." A violent shiver cut through him.

An elderly woman was descending into the Court, her back ramrod straight and her cane umbrella hooked into the ropes: riding the swaying cradle just as casually as if it were a bright red no. 24 Edinburgh bus.

"I am Lady Ives o' the Blackhill!" Her imperious voice rang out. "I am Isobel Ives! I believe you've been looking for me. Now will someone tell me what all this nonsense is about?"

To Cameron's horror, his gran was back from the dead.

CHAPTER 8

FALSE WITNESS

A vision of the last time he'd seen his gran – her face twisted into a snarl as she tumbled into darkness – flashed into Cameron's mind. His hand went automatically to his midriff: the site of a scar that had formed supernaturally fast that same night. Inside him lurked a deeper wound that he knew would never heal.

She'd betrayed him and his dad. He could never forgive her.

He sank back in his cradle.

"I'm lost."

"I don't understand," the lamp whispered. "I thought you needed her to win?"

"I might get to keep the shop – but if she's back, that doesn't matter. It'll be the least of my worries." The creaking rope-cradle drew level. Everything about the tall, thin figure was horribly familiar. "I might've known she'd survive. If anyone could, it'd be her. She always found a way to hang on..."

The judge's bat-nose snuffled, alert to the new arrival. "It seems your case is void, Mr Grey. In the matter of 'who has the lady?', the answer is: 'the defence'."

"But you promised. You said she wouldn't be a problem," Dr Black whined.

Grey made a dismissive gesture and Black lapsed into silence. They both seemed as surprised as Cameron by the sudden appearance of Grandma Ives.

"On the contrary, my Lord," Grey blustered. "There is no evidence that this... person is the woman in question."

"There isn't? We'll see about that." The old woman rummaged in her bag and drew out a red booklet that she held open. "My passport! Not the most recent likeness, I'll admit, but no one could deny it is me." She touched her coiffured hair and sniffed. "In my prime."

"Human frippery! Inadmissible!"

"My grandson will identify me too," the old woman added. "Or are you going to start to cast doubt over his identity as well?"

Cameron stared through the smoky air. The last thing he wanted was a family reunion with his scary-mad grandma, but he couldn't let Grey win either. *If he acknowledged her, what was he getting himself into?*

"Well, Cameron? Tell them who I am."

"Mr Duffy," Grey said, flecks of spit speckling his lawyer's robes, "doesn't seem entirely certain..."

There was a curious flicker in the old woman's eyes. "The poor boy," she said pointedly, "is clearly overcome with emotion. It's been so long since we've seen each other, and he was quite *heartbroken* when I had to go away. He begged me to stay... as I'm sure he remembers *only too well*."

That wasn't right... Cameron rubbed his forehead. There was something going on – but he had no idea what. He glanced at Grey. The odious daemon was clutching the rim of his prosecutor's box, breathing heavily, waiting for any fumble he could seize upon.

"No, that's her." Cameron swallowed, wondering what he was getting into. "My gran. Grandma Ives. The one we've all been looking for."

"You see? Poor lad. This has all been a great strain on him." The old woman held up a powdery hand, forestalling Grey's response. "If the Court will not take the word of two members of a distinguished Parallel family, would you question the testimony of Lord Janus himself?"

There were murmurs from the jury at the mention of the Portal God.

"No, I thought not. There are any number of Important Daemonic Personages I could call upon to vouchsafe my identity. Such are the advantages of being a premier Parallel trader of many years standing." A thin smile spread across the old woman's lips. "I put it to the Court: I am Isobel Ives – whether you like it or not."

"I would question it!" Grey exploded, his chins

quivering with indignation. "I knew Ms Ives. I had the great misfortune of dealing with the harridan on several occasions, and Madam, *you are not her!*"

The old woman's eyebrows arched. "How very strange. I have no recollection of you at all." She leant forward in her rope cradle and studied the shaking daemon. "I think I'd remember such a colossal bore."

The jury erupted into laughter; wolfish yelps mixed with Cervidae snorts and all manner of strange shrieks and cries.

"My Lord, I must protest," Grey began, but Grandma Ives checked her wristwatch and patted her face as if covering a yawn, which only seemed to drive the jury to greater hysteria.

Cameron clenched his fists, his fingernails biting into his palms, dumbstruck by her performance. He honestly didn't know whether to laugh or cry. The old woman caught his eye and, to his amazement, gave him the tiniest of half-winks.

What the Parallel *was going on?*

"ENOUGH!" The judge's gavel slammed into the lectern, its percussive beat silencing the chattering Court. "The defence claims we have the woman – the prosecution argues not. There is a way to prove this." His mouth opened wide, revealing black and red ridges, and he licked his lips with his shrivelled tongue. "There must be a test of blood."

"Oh dear." The lamp turned orange. "You'd be amazed how often it comes down to that."

"What does he mean?" Cameron asked. "He's not gonna bite her?"

"It's simple. The bloodlines of the human and daemon clans that descend from Mitchell and Astredo's covens – those present at the World Split – are well known. It is those families who carry the Parallel Inheritance, and it is their activities this Court oversees. If your witness is who she claims to be, his Honour will know it."

The old woman however didn't seem particularly pleased at the judge's proposal. She tugged at the rope cradle with her umbrella, as if hoping to trigger the mechanism that would lift her out of Court. "Now really, is this necessary? Nobody said anything to me about a blood test."

"This will settle it." The judge's fangs protruded further. "Finally and irrevocably. Bring her to me!"

Overhead, the winches started to clank. With a great shuddering jerk, Grandma Ives' cradle began to shift. She clapped her hand to her head and Cameron blinked. It looked for a moment as if her great silver tower of hair had temporarily slipped sideways...

As the cradle moved horizontally across the airspace of the Court, it drew closer to Cameron and the old woman met his gaze directly. He had a sudden start of recognition, and let out a stifled yelp.

It wasn't Grandma Ives at all –
It was Eve!

Eve – dressed in his gran's old clothes, her face

lacquered in thick white make-up: an elaborate network of fine lines etched with eyebrow pencil around her eyes and mouth. In the dingy, smoke-filled Court he'd been utterly taken in.

"What – are – you – doing?" he stuttered as her cradle swung past.

"Trying to save us all, what do you think?" she hissed back.

"Some kind of *warning* would've been good – before you went all Halloween and dragged up as Evil-Zombie-Grandma!"

"Well forgive me," she said icily, "I was going to tell you properly. How was I to know I was gonna get zapped off Janus's train by a magic doorway – and end up back in Scott and Forceworthy's cellar? At least I left a note!"

"Note? What note? I didn't get any note?"

There was another groan from the winches, and the cradle took a further lurch across the pit.

"Well, I left one! That nasty lump started bleating at me as soon as I got back, so there was no time to lose. I had to go find all this stuff." She flicked her hand, indicating her disguise.

Cameron swore. "The lump! I bet it ate it. It already scrobbled our answerphone, so it must've munched that as well..."

"Doesn't matter," said Eve. "It didn't work anyway. I'm going to get bitten by bat-face." She gave the ropes a frantic shake. "Cameron, I'm proper scared. Will we still be friends if I go all blood-sucky?"

"My Lord Justice, you can't just bite her!" Cameron shouted. "It's not fair!"

"It will decide the issue of identity beyond any reasonable doubt."

"You won't even like her! I bet she tastes awful – all old and mean and bad-tempered!"

Eve shot Cameron a look. *"Really?"*

He rolled his shoulders. *Best I could come up with...*

The judge gave a dry cough. "Gratified as I am by your concern, you need have no fear. I require only a sample – not a full vein to draw on." He held out a long pin in his claw-like hand. A gargoyle daemon swooped down, seized it and flew it over to Eve. "My 'select condition' will not be passed on."

Eve hesitated, her face pale, the sharp tip of the pin poised above her finger.

"See how she resists," Grey crowed. "She knows her deception will be uncovered! I trust the Court will prosecute this false and treacherous witness to the very limits of the law."

"Oh shut up, you horrible thing." Eve closed her eyes, and with a tiny shudder pressed the pin into her flesh. A bright red spot of blood sprang out, staining the metal. The gargoyle snatched the pin from her and returned it to the judge's hand.

"If this woman descends from Mistress Agnes Ives O' the Black Hill, late of Mitchell's coven, I will know it. Blood will always out." The judge sniffed at the steel instrument with evident relish. His claw gestured in the air. "The witness may be removed.

This is all I require."

The winches began to clatter again, and Eve's cradle started to ascend. "Sorry," she mouthed to Cameron.

"Don't be! It was a magnificent try!" he called as the cradle swung up and out of view.

All eyes in the Court turned to the judge. Delicately, as if about to savour a rare wine, he stuck the pin into his mouth.

Cameron's chest went tight. Eve had no family connection to him or Gran. She was just a friend, someone he'd stumbled upon and helped escape from the clutches of Mrs Ferguson. There was no way this could turn out right. He wished Morgan were here. One of his lopsided grins would be awesomely reassuring.

What would he say?

"Any ideas how to get out of this one, Shorty?"

"I was thinking we could suddenly develop the power of flight."

"Top notion. Let me know how that works out."

The wolf-boy was skilled at getting out of tight corners – but even he would balk at a breakout attempt from a net swinging over a pit.

"Interesting." The judge drew the pin slowly from his mouth and gave it a final lick. "The generations have had an influence... the Parallel Inheritance is diluted by the presence of other human families, its unique flavour altered. Nonetheless," he set the pin down delicately, "this is undoubtedly the

Ives bloodline. I know it. I am thus satisfied this woman is Isobel Ives. She lives, so the tenancy of the shop remains unchanged. Mr Grey, your client has lost."

Cameron exhaled hard, letting out acres of tension with a rush. This was the second time in recent minutes his mind had been blown. *How could the judge get it so wrong?* Not that he was about to raise an objection... He hurriedly composed his face. "Good. I'm glad. Now, can I please go home?"

"I won't have this!" Dr Black shouted. "Grey, what are you going to do about this travesty?"

"My Lord, I must protest –"

"Must you, Grey?"

Grey swelled to his full height, his belly toppling over the edge of the box that held him. "This human is clearly not Lady Ives, as anyone can see –"

"I rely on subtler senses," the judge snarled. "The case is dismissed."

Dr Black's cradle began to rise, its occupant ranting about injustice. Grey however remained where he was. His swollen fists clenched and he began to shake.

A vibration ran through the court. The air stirred and the temperature seemed to drop by several degrees. Cameron took a tighter hold of his cradle. *Was it his imagination, or was it swaying more than before?*

He glanced up at the guide ropes. The winch mechanisms were creaking and groaning like ships' rigging caught in a gathering storm. There was a sudden crunch of gears that echoed round the chasm.

112

Seconds later: a corresponding twang of something shearing free from its moorings.

For a moment, everything seemed frozen – then loose rope whiplashed past and the jury box tipped sideways, suspended now only by two of its corners. The occupants yelled and screamed as they tried frantically to stay onboard the slanting container. Those that could got clear: the fey woman leapt into flight and the light column simply vanished. The metal beetle's carapace cracked open, revealing a helicopter-like propeller. It whirred upwards, but two of the jurors – who had no other means of escape – jumped for its legs and grabbed on, trying to hitch a lift. Their combined weight was too much for the insect: the propeller sputtered, and all three spiralled down.

"The jury are released from duty." The judge's leathery wings unfurled luxuriantly, his fangs glinting. "Their services are no longer required." He took to the air, heading downwards in close pursuit of the fallen jurors.

Another creaking judder resonated through the court. More ropes started to ping and snap. Cameron's faithful lamp plunged out of sight.

"Weir! No!" he shouted, as the flickering glow dwindled into darkness.

The rope net around him started to give and the cradle dropped sickeningly by a couple of metres before jerking taut again. The lattice was unravelling, coming apart like a string bag pulled by a loose thread.

He reached up, grabbing the main rope with all his might.

"You're doing this, aren't you? It's all you!" he yelled at Grey.

Grey was exultant, his box alone still secure upon its ropes. He was riding the swinging container gleefully, in the manner of a pirate king sailing into battle. "Problems will be absorbed, young sir! And if they can't be absorbed, they will simply be removed!"

Only a single rope was left in Cameron's hands. The cradle was entirely unknotted, its strands flailing loosely around him. He could feel his grip slipping. The wind whipped past, raging and howling in his ears...

CHAPTER 9

OUTSIDE THE FAT MOON

The sides of the cavern were too far away. Even if he could've leapt the distance, the ancient walls were slick with slime, and footholds far from plentiful.

Cameron focussed instead on the rope that was creeping through his hands, centimetre by painful centimetre. Close up, its design was surprisingly complex: composed of numerous tiny fibres interwoven and whorled around each other.

Without questioning the instinct that drove him, he thrust his chin forward and snapped his jaws tight. The rope tasted bitter, its threads impregnated with ancient tar. His hands flexed afresh, somehow finding a traction they had previously lacked.

"Hold on, mate! We've got you!" a voice boomed and, with a yank, the rope began to move. In fits and starts he was dragged upwards. Grey's manic laughter choked off as his opponent was snatched away.

Cameron spun, rotating swiftly clockwise then anticlockwise and back again, but, anchored by both teeth and hands, he clung on.

Rock walls turned to close-packed brick and then to wooden panels. At last he was approaching the top of the pit.

"That's it! You're nearly there!" Eve's head appeared over the edge, freed from her grandiose silver wig. Her hands flew to her mouth and she turned to her unseen companion. *"Morgan!* He's gone –"

"I know! Ignore it. We've got to keep turning!"

"But look at him!"

"What did I say? *TURN!*"

The rope started to lift faster. At last it was all reeled in, swallowed onto the winch's spindle. Two pairs of arms seized Cameron and pulled him over the balustrade. He tumbled to the ground in a heap of aching limbs.

He whooped in delight and grinned broadly at his rescuers, and started to say how good it was to see them, but his mouth didn't seem to work, and his tongue got snagged up on his teeth. Rough palms pressed either side of his face. Morgan's green eyes burned, his familiar scent surprisingly close. Cameron tried to say *"What are you doing?"* but the only sound he could form was a startled yelp.

"Listen," Morgan spoke calmly, "there's no moon

116

right now. Do you hear me? It's daytime. The next Fat Moon is a month away. Do you understand?"

"Have you gone mental or something?"

Cameron tried to retort, but instead let out a bass-heavy rumble from deep within his chest. He shoved hard at Morgan to make him back off. As his hands made contact, he realised they weren't hands at all – *they were paws.*

He shot backwards, pulling free from Morgan's grip.

"Hey, hey, hey! Relax!" Morgan said urgently. "You're partway to becoming a wolf. You know that now. Your head and your forearms have shifted. But it's all right! You can still come back. You've just got to focus."

"Vow...cus?" Cameron's voice was a throaty growl.

"Yeah. You've gotta concentrate. Remember how I taught you? You've gotta think human-shaped thoughts. See the things you can only do when you're in that body: like reading a book, or using your fingers to play videogames, or shaping the chords on your guitar. Forget about the chase, and how you feel so strong you could run for always, free and wild."

"Morgan, I don't think you're helping." Eve reached out and touched Cameron's arm where the black wolf fur had broken through his shirt. "It's ok, Cameron. You don't need to run. You're safe. Think about us. Think about home."

He tried to do as she said but adrenaline was surging through his body. His eyes narrowed and he sniffed the air, detecting the telltale trace of the Greys. He wanted to deal with them, to hunt them down...

"*The... reys? Wha... bout... the... reys?*"

"Scarpered," said Morgan. "They had control for a while, but the Weir lamps came zooming in with backup: the biggest bull daemons you've ever seen! Proper mad minotaurs, beating the Greys back with sticks and ropes, and tearing them away from the winches. It was pretty awesome, actually..."

"Again, not so much with the helping." Eve shot Morgan a look. "The point is: they're gone. You're with us. You can be Cameron again. Not the wolf."

He met her eyes and she nodded encouragingly. "Trust me."

A shiver rippled through him and his skin contracted, as if he was being flung from the heat of a summer's day into a bracing shower. He felt his muscles tighten and his bones start to shift. The fur retreated from his hands. He touched his face, feeling it flatten out, moulding into its familiar human shape and leaving behind the pointed muzzle of his wolf-self.

"It – keeps – happening." He stretched his jaw. "I didn't even notice myself shift that time. How is that possible?"

"Shouldn't be. Not outside the Fat Moon." Morgan had an odd expression on his face, somewhere between jealousy and fear. "Not in the Human World and not on the Parallel. Down in Daemonic, maybe, if you were a full-blooded werewolf... But you're not."

Cameron slanted a glance at him. "Maybe I'm turning into one?"

Morgan shook his head. "Doesn't work like that. You've got to be born to it. Not like you. You're a human. You just got bit."

"Bit by you."

"Yeah, I know." The wolf-boy turned away, and walked to the side of the pit. He folded his arms and leant upon the balustrade, his face lit by the reddish glow from below. "Like I'm ever gonna forget."

Cameron hurried after him. "But don't you see… it's ok? My wolf-side saved me. It keeps saving me. It's how I escaped the train when the Greys attacked, and how I got rid of that Weaver. It's a *good* thing. Without it, I'd be dead."

"It is what it is, mate." Morgan shook his head. "But this is just gonna make the pack more interested, and they've already got a nose on. Once they get fixed on something, they don't ever let it go."

Eve frowned. "What are you talking about?"

"They know all about Cameron," said Morgan. "I'd better tell you two what happened after you left Janus's train…

"Those grey blob-things went clambering over the Temple carriage. I could hear them thumping about on the roof like a couple of extra-fat seagulls. I kept yelling, telling Janus he had to do something, but he just ignored me. Sips his wine, dead calm, like nothing was going on.

"There was this metal scream from the engine, and

we start to slow right down. We were in Daemonic by then – I'd felt us leave the Parallel. I roared at that two-faced twit, said he had to take me back.

"'That would be difficult,' he says. 'A vital part of the January Express has been stolen. It will be a little time before the train runs again.'

"'Stolen? You just let them take it!' I shouted. 'You didn't even try to fight back!'

"His other face gives me this crafty look and says, 'Be calm, my stout little wolf-heart. The time for action will come. For now, you have the Omniclavis – the all-key. I suggest you use it to *unlock* the mystery.'

"Then he waves his hand like he's ordering another drink and this trapdoor opens up under me. 'Ciao,' he says, 'or should I say, see you later?', and before I know it, I'm flat on my face in the snow beneath the train..."

Eve sniggered but Morgan pressed on.

"I was deep in pack territory, and it wasn't long before I got picked up by a patrol. Had to go and do a bit of bowing and scraping. Let the old girl re-assert her status as Top Dog. Made me listen to a long boring speech about duty. She wasn't pleased I'd bargained away that manky bone debt. Turns out she thought I only had it on a loan." Morgan grinned lopsidedly. "More fool her."

"Woah, woah," said Cameron. "Back up. Who's the 'old girl' and why does she get the bowing and the scraping?"

"Yeah, well." Morgan rubbed the back of his head and looked bashful. "She's my mum, isn't she? She's sort of pack leader. Like the, um, Wolf Queen."

Cameron and Eve stared at him. Morgan shrugged. "Told you she was fierce. She thinks she owns me – just like all the other Were-kind on the Edinburgh Parallel. I mean, by tradition it's her hubby who leads, as he's the Alpha Male. But everyone knows she's the real power."

"How very progressive," said Eve lightly.

"I don't make the stupid rules, do I? If I was interested in pack politics I'd still be there, making out like I was the dutiful son and heir. Ha! Like I'd want that!" Morgan snorted and scratched the side of his face. "That's not the worst of it though. Turns out the Brain-Dead Biker blabbed. Grant gave her the full download on Cam-boy and now she wants to meet him."

"What's the problem with that?" said Eve. "Cameron can be very charming when he wants to be. I'm sure he'll win them over..."

"Don't you get it?" Morgan looked exasperated. "Lone wolves aren't tolerated. The pack doesn't want any randoms who could act out – shifting and rampaging about – getting the humans to notice we exist. And if Cam can shift at will – even in the Human World – that's something new and risky. They're not gonna like it."

"Oh dear." Eve waved a finger at Cameron. "Morgan's mum won't like you. Whatever will you do?"

Now it was Eve's turn to be stared at by the two boys. "Oh your faces! Bother the stupid wolves. Are we not forgetting one tiny thing? We won! We won the case." She did a little step and dance on the spot. "We beat Grey and Black. We saw them off! And we get to keep the shop now. Of course, it's all due to my brilliance, you two shouldn't get any credit."

Cameron started to smile. "She's right, you know. Rude but right. We won because of Eve and her mad disguise. Although it's a bit down to that vamp judge as well... Why the *Parallel* did he think we were related?"

"I dunno. I could buy it." Morgan said, glancing from Cameron to Eve. He ducked from a playfully swung fist. "Ow! Get off! What are you hitting me for?"

"Because that's the worst thing you've ever said," said Cameron. "Still it was a genius idea of Eve's. How did you think of it?"

Eve glowed with pleasure. "Remember we told your friend Amy we were cousins? She totally bought it. I do look a tiny bit like you. And I had an old photo of your gran to copy from. It wasn't so difficult, once I found the wig and clothes."

"You did the voice as well," said Cameron, "and the attitude. I really thought she was back."

Eve ran a hand through her hair, smoothing it out. "I've spent the past year playing the grown-up and sort of standing in for her. It wasn't too much of a stretch."

Cameron shook his head. "I can't believe you got away with it."

"A disbelief I share."

They turned to see Dr Black watching them from the shadows. He seemed to have calmed right down since he was hauled out of the pit ranting and raving, but it was clear he was not at all happy. "The girl's disguise was pure pantomime, but the blood-type duplication... that must've taken planning. I wouldn't have thought you had the skills."

Eve gave a tight smile, admitting nothing. "You shouldn't underestimate us."

"A fair point," said Dr Black mildly. "It's not a mistake I'll make again."

"Are you looking for your fat friend?" said Cameron. "Because he's still swinging around in the Court. I suppose it's too much to hope he's stuck down there."

Dr Black's mouth twitched and his eyes went dead for a second. "Mr Grey doesn't get stuck anywhere. He'll find a way to leech himself out. He always does."

"What is it with you and him?" Cameron persisted. "Because if he's got some kind of hold over you, *tell us*. We don't have to be enemies. We could help."

"Hold? On me? Don't be ridiculous... I've a first-class mind. As if some cellar daemon could..."

"You should listen to him," Eve added. "Believe me, I've been there. I know what it's like to have a daemon wedged inside your head. I know what it can do."

Black's expression hardened. "There's no hold. Grey works for me." He pulled his mobile out his pocket and stabbed at the screen. "This isn't over. Using the Court was only one option. Don't think I'm beaten."

"I don't get it," said Cameron. "Why are you doing this? Why don't you let it go? Do you hate us so much?"

"Hate you?" Black's eyebrow raised. "You're an irrelevance. Merely something in the way of a greater experiment." Holding his glowing phone aloft, he stalked away into the gloomy corridors.

"Nothing about that guy makes sense," Cameron muttered. "What experiment? What's he after, *really?*"

"We should follow and find out." Morgan rubbed a palm against his fist. "I reckon it's time we went on the offensive."

"Yes, all very butch," said Eve. "But we haven't got a lamp to guide us. He could be heading anywhere. This building's like a maze."

"*Lamp*, she says. What do we need a lamp for?" Morgan tapped his nose. "Best tracker in town, this. Come on. Follow me!"

CHAPTER 10

THE WORLD ENGINE

They moved through the Court, Morgan scenting Black's progress. Here and there they saw signs of the Greys' attack on the winch room, and their subsequent retreat: doors hung off their hinges and Weir lamps lay smashed and guttering. A sullen bull daemon pushed past, grunting and rubbing at a broken-off horn, and every so often they encountered a space where something was simply missing.

"Gobbled by the Greys?" said Eve, and Cameron nodded.

The absences chafed, like grit in a shoe. He could feel his wolf-side was restless, stirring somewhere at the back of his mind, uttering frustrated little whines and snarls.

Not now. Not yet...

He clenched his fists then glanced down, thinking

another subconscious shift might be on the way. He caught Eve watching, and shoved his hands in his pockets.

"You'd let me know if there was a problem, right? With the wolf?" Eve spoke quietly while Morgan sniffed on ahead. "Because I worry about you, you know."

"*You* worry about *me*?" Cameron remembered the little girl he'd first encountered under the thrall of the daemonic Mrs Ferguson. She'd been resourceful, but scared and brittle as well. She'd changed so much in the past year. "Are you sure that's the right way round?"

"Sometimes it is," she said, and gave his arm a squeeze.

"Hush up," said Morgan. "This is where the trail stops."

At the end of a dusty corridor stood a frosted-glass door, the darkened panel showing no signs of activity within.

Painted lettering in a gothic font read:

Hogg & Stevenson – Barristers at Law
DECEASED   **& Grey**

'& Grey' had been appended below in a modern style, and 'DECEASED' added in block capitals beneath the name of Hogg.

"Looks like the right place." Cameron tested the handle. "But I guess we stop here too – unless we can force it?"

126

"Forgetting something?" Morgan dangled a brass key in front of Cameron's nose. "We've got an Access All Areas pass, courtesy of a certain two-faced deity."

Eve snatched it smartly. "I get first shot." As the key neared the door, its metal prongs stretched and reshaped. It slid gracefully into the lock and turned with a satisfying click.

"That was underwhelming," she said. "I was hoping for sparkles."

"Never mind the special effects." Cameron pushed the door, which opened smoothly. "It worked."

Beyond lay a cluttered office. Three high stools stood behind tall desks. On the wall, a portrait of a lugubrious boar daemon in a lawyer's wig and robes radiated disapproval over the room.

"The late Mr Hogg, I presume," said Eve, studying the portrait. "Do you think Grey gobbled him too?"

"Absorbed, more like. I wonder if that's how he got to be a lawyer?" Eve slanted Cameron a glance and he continued, "You know that answer machine the lump ate? It started speaking with clicks and gurgles afterwards, like it had sort of taken on part of the machine."

"Interesting. I wonder what Grey's absorbed from Black? What kind of doctor is Black, anyway?" She stuck out her tongue and pulled a face. "I wouldn't go see him. He'd probably prescribe acid."

"I don't think he's a medic. I think he's a scientist. He said something about us being in the way of his 'great experiment'."

"If you two have finished playing the Dynamic Detective Duo, you'd better get over here." Morgan gestured to a door in the far wall. "And *keep it down*. I can hear 'em talking."

Cameron hurried over. "Hold up before you use the Omniclavis. It only works three times –"

"I know! I can count!" Morgan turned the handle. "No need. It's open."

The door gave onto the upper balcony of a private library. They crept through, staying hunkered to the ground, and beneath the level of the balustrade. On the level below, three deep wingchairs were arranged around a fireplace. Dr Black sat in the one facing towards them, his legs crossed, apparently engrossed in his phone.

"With you in a moment, Watt," he addressed the chair opposite. "This message won't send, and I've got the department on my back again. My reputation is riding on this. Can't you get decent wifi down here?"

"We try, but the signal gets eaten. There is a species of daemonic metal beetle that finds radio waves irresistible."

As Black's companion spoke, a steady stream of smoke issued through the peak of a blackened-tin top hat, which was all that could be seen of the chair's occupant. A rhythmic wheeze was heard, pitched somewhere between the mechanised breathing of a hospital ventilator and the chuffing of a resting steam engine.

"Yes, everything has a predator, I know," said Black.

"I respect that, even if it's inconvenient. There's a pleasing circularity to the equation." He dropped his phone onto the arm of his chair.

"It is in the nature of flesh life," his companion said. "And it holds true for metal life as well."

"Metal life! I know all about metal life, and it's unreliable," said Black. "There's always some bug in the system. Something to hold me back."

"You know nothing. Your computers, your phones, your technologies are but pale imitations of what they could be; machines without souls. When the Makaris built me, they gave me life *proper*. It is to honour their memory that I do this work."

The Makaris. Up on the balcony, Cameron shivered. The Makaris were an ancient daemon clan of engineers, supposed to be long extinct. Thanks to his gran's ill-fated plans, he'd previously encountered two of the artefacts they'd left behind, and only just escaped with his life.

"Three years we've been working on the World Engine," Dr Black jabbed a scornful finger at his companion. "Three years you've assured me it just needs one more part, one more adjustment, one more sacrifice – and then it'll run. But still it doesn't work. Well, I'm tired of waiting."

"Your impatience is not required. It will not mend the machine."

"Was that supposed to be a joke?"

"It's a statement." The regular chuffing, halting breath paced up. "The World Engine is old and complicated. The governor valve from the January Express has proved to be compatible, but still... there are problems."

"Why won't it go?" Black snarled. "Tell me!"

"It is as you suspected. The medium the Engine was built to work upon has changed. When the World Split forged the Parallel, it was a no place: a void, an inter-dimensional gap. That is what the Engine was designed for. For three hundred years the Engine has lain dormant, and during that time the Parallel has filled with activity and life..."

"That boy and his erratic friends." Black got up, took a decanter of amber liquid from the mantelpiece and poured himself a drink. "They mingle. They move between. They cause chaos. Why can't they just stay put?"

"By constantly crossing the boundaries they generate dimensional instability, so re-enforcing the Parallel's existence. And so... the Engine will not run."

Cameron exchanged a glance with Morgan. "Black wasn't lying," he hissed. "This isn't about us. His plan covers the entire Parallel."

Eve nudged him, "Look."

With the sound of antiquated clockwork ticking into life, Black's colleague rose from his chair. As he crossed the room, it became clear Watt's entire body was as metallic as the steaming top-hat vent attached to his head. A curved tin plate covered his face, with rivets indicating eyebrows and moustache, a slit for a mouth and two orange lamps in place of eyes. Pistons articulated his arms and legs, and an inspection port set in his chest revealed a series of valves clustered around a padlock-shaped heart. The complex parts pumped furiously and glinted in the firelight.

"I will see if Grey has collected himself." The mechanical man pulled a rope, causing a set of wooden shutters to concertina open. Beyond lay a dank rock wall that must have backed onto the Court pit. A network of pipes ran in through the wall from many directions, all heading to a voluminous glass collecting-jar. Glutinous grey liquid dripped through the pipes and a familiar sugary-mushroom stink seeped into the air.

Watt attached a rubber tube to the side of the flask and handed the mouthpiece to Black. "Did you hear that, Grey? The World Engine needs a void to work on. We must abandon the Court, and take direct action."

"But of course, Sir. This is most gratifying. My wish is, as ever, to expand." A bubbling, multiple voice responded, as if Grey's crawling tones had been duplicated many times over. "My sub-forms are currently being collated and re-absorbed. New matter has been drawn in as well. I will shortly be ready to spore."

A thick grey pustule pushed to the surface of the churning grey liquid.

"Such a world I've found, that has things like you in it." Dr Black put a hand over his mouth, and for a minute looked decidedly queasy. "Sometimes I think I should've turned back when I had the chance."

"Oh no, sir. Never say that," the legion of voices wheedled. "Your experiment would be incomplete, the theory unproved, and you'd always wonder... No one would get to know the discoveries of the great Dr Alasdair Black."

"Three hundred years the Engine has waited." Watt's valves chugged and pumped. "I will not let anything stand in the way of its glorious activation."

Black drew out a handkerchief and mopped his forehead. "I made a deal with the devil when I took you on, Grey."

"No, sir. Not the devil. Just a resourceful daemon," the grey pustule at the top of the flask swelled, puffing out into a crude replica of Mr Grey's face, "who *yearns* to do your bidding..."

Black shut his eyes, breathing heavily. "Very well. I give you permission. Spore and multiply. Go out into the Parallel. Empty it – and shut it down."

CHAPTER 11

NIGHT IS FALLING

Cameron, Morgan and Eve set up makeshift beds made from old blankets at the front of Scott & Forceworthy's music shop. They wanted to be as far away from the dome-covered lump as possible. It was like having a spy in the building, Eve said, but, as Morgan pointed out, at least they knew where it was – and what it was up to.

"It's either stay here with the lump," Cameron had said, "or go back to the house with Weavers and whatever else might try to gatecrash..."

Faced with that choice, they had decided to spend an uncomfortable night on the floor. Each had taken it in turns to keep watch while the other two slept, but the lump had showed no signs of stirring.

The next morning, Cameron tentatively lifted the dome while Eve brandished a claymore she'd dug out

133

the storeroom, and Morgan hefted a fire extinguisher. The lump appeared inactive: pale grey and wizened like an ancient mushroom.

"Perhaps it's dead," Eve said. "It was only a baby one. Just a lump of chin really."

"Don't go feeling sorry for it." Morgan lowered the fire extinguisher. "It's still part of Grey."

She nodded and poked the lump with her sword. It parted around the sword's tip, but the blade came out intact. "I think the energy's gone out of it. If we wait a bit longer, we might be able to scrape it off the desk." She gave an amused snort. "Like an enormous dried-out bogey."

"I don't even know what you mean," said Cameron in a monotone.

"As if!"

"I don't like it. If this one's powered down, that must mean Grey's active somewhere else." Cameron frowned. They'd snuck away from Hogg's chambers as the Grey morass seethed and churned, not certain how long they would have before the flask's contents burst out... "If we're gonna stop the Greys and save the Parallel, I need to know what they're up to."

"Do *we* have to save the Parallel, then?" Eve looked doubtful. "Is that what we do? I mean, I want to – but I don't exactly think we're superheroes."

"Yeah. Just two werewolves, and the Girl who Grew Up in her Sleep." Morgan raised an eyebrow. "Really ordinary. Bit boring, maybe."

"You know what I mean! We're just us. Eve and

Cameron and Morgan, and our little shop. I was hoping it would go back to normal if we stopped the Court." Eve bit her lip. "Daft, I guess."

"If Grey and Black manage to shut down the Parallel, there *is* no business," Cameron said. "Don't you see? What happens then? I'd have to go back to school, try and get a proper job, and you – I don't even know where they'd try and make you go. And what about Morgan? If the Parallel goes, he might get stuck in Daemonic with the pack."

"Morgan says, 'stuff the pack'. Bunch of over-trained Yes Dogs." Morgan scratched at his neck and squinted. "Reckon I belong here."

"Thanks, man." Cameron shot the blond wolf-boy a grateful glance. "So, you see? We've got to fight back. We can't let this happen."

Eve hesitated. "Yes, you're right. I think I just needed to hear you say it." She patted both boys on their shoulders. "Ok, Super-Team. Where do we start?"

They all met back at the shop later that same afternoon. Cameron could instantly tell from the expression on his friends' faces they'd all seen the same thing.

"It's too late, isn't it?" he said, "It's already happened."

Taking a seat on a trombone case, Eve leant forward and began her story. "I went to the daemon market down in the Cowgate. You and Morgan had always made it sound so lively and charming: all the paper lanterns, the smells of frying food, the stall-holders singing out, selling their wares…"

"Load of shonky rip-offs and dodgy-curry merchants," Morgan rumbled. "Sooner cut your throat than give you a discount."

"Was it? I wouldn't know." Eve smiled sadly. "It's gone. The stalls are empty, and the lanterns are all torn down. There was just one seller left – an old selkie woman, frantically packing her charms into a bundle. She nearly jumped out of her whiskery skin when she saw me.

"'Ach, they're all awa', dearie. Packed and run awa'. Couldna stand up to they grey bogles.'

"She glanced around and beckoned me closer. Her breath was pretty bad – like rotten seaweed.

"'Wicked things like that, they lurk and spread. Start off as a mouldy smell at the back o' yer cupboard, and you pay no heed. Before you know it, they've got a hold, and nothin' ye can do will shift 'em.'

"She put a fishbone charm in my hand and said I should wear it for protection.

"'I'm awa' back to the shore. I'll put ma seal face on, swim out into the water, and look for a wee island to take shelter on. There's no place in the Parallel for the likes o' me now.'"

Eve pulled the charm out and showed it to the boys: a translucent network of thin bones had been woven into a medallion.

136

Morgan made a disgusted noise. "For all the good that'll do, you might as well hang a fish supper round your neck."

"Don't laugh, Morgan. She was terrified. She's too old to survive out in the North Sea for long, this time of year. The Parallel is her home." Eve put the bone charm down. "And that's not all. It was getting dark as the old creature left, but it wasn't like a regular winter's night at all. It was as if the whole marketplace was turning fuzzy and fading out... I didn't like it. I shifted back to the Human World and came home." Eve's face paled and she wrapped her arms around her body. "I don't know what might've happened if I'd stayed."

"Yeah. Not good." Morgan shuffled on his improvised packing-case seat. "I saw something like that as well...

"I started by heading for Kitty's Tavern, to listen for the latest gossip, you know? But none of the doors were working – they're all blocked off, even the one hidden under Greyfriars' Bobby. Looks like everyone's running scared – even things that were pretty scary to begin with. The Temperatori's shrine hasn't got an egg on it, the Joyful People of the Banner are lookin' grim, and the Portobello Pleasure Gardens have turned post-apocalyptic. They're all emptying out – and shutting down. I thought I'd go see Marlene as a last resort."

"Oh?" said Eve lightly. "Who is Marlene?"

"Och, you know, the fey trader. Big on glamour,

low on integrity. Hangs out in that upside-down tenement beneath the Royal Mile. I was climbing the rope ladder, thinking *aye, aye, it's pretty dark down here,* when I pass her fluttering off in the opposite direction. She screeches at me as she swoops by, 'Night is falling, wolf kin. If you had any sense in your dog-skull you'd leave before it all goes black.' And that's when I realise – the tenement's gone. It's not there! There's nothing but me and a ladder, and that's starting to look glitched-up as well...

"So I got out sharpish."

"Montmorency's leaving too," said Cameron, taking up the tale. The half-daemon shopkeeper was an old ally of his, based on a dislike of Cameron's scheming grandmother. "He said he'd had some 'heavy-handed persuasion' to go. Says he's heading to France to wait it out.

"I asked how that'd help. I mean, doesn't the Parallel run there as well?

"'Course it does, lad. *"Le Parallèle Diabolique,"* the French daemons call it. Think they invented it too. Well, they're welcome to it – I'll be staying clear. It's time I took a holiday anyway. I've got enough money saved to last me till June. I'll be ok – unless this thing spreads on out.'

"'How can it spread?' I asked.

"'Parallel's all connected, isn't it? Starts at the fissure point in Edinburgh, and runs right through the heart of the Human and Daemon Worlds.' And Montmorency slapped at his chest. 'Touches those of us with the Inheritance as well. Start messing about with it, you don't know what'll happen.'

"He picked up his suitcases, locked the door of his shop, and looked up at the sky like he was checking for rain. 'Reckon I'll get a few months in the sun before it's all over.' He reached into his shoulder bag, and handed me his netbook. 'Here, what do I need this for, weighing me down? You take care of it, lad, till I'm back, eh? Don't go crashing my high score on *Monster Roller Derby*, or hacking my emails.'

"Then he put on his dark glasses to cover up his daemon eye, pulled down his bobble hat, and was away down the road..."

Cameron drew the computer from his backpack. Morgan looked at it hopefully. "Any good? Bet his tunes are rubbish."

"I didn't look at them. His new netbook, though... why would he give it away?" Cameron shook his head. "He's acting like he's not coming back."

Cameron had planned to explore further on the Parallel, but the closer he got to Grey's devastation, the more the wolf in his head became uneasy, whining and howling like a nagging headache.

He massaged his temples. "Morgan, what do you do when the wolf won't lie quiet?"

"How do you mean, mate?" Morgan's brow furrowed.

"You know. When it won't shut up?"

"I don't follow. The wolf is you. You are the wolf." Morgan sat back and crossed his arms over his chest.

"Unless you're asking – how do I stop worrying about things? And the answer to that is – I don't worry." He grinned rakishly. "Things are what they are. You gotta make the best of them."

"Such wisdom from one so scruffy," said Eve.

Morgan shrugged. "Works for me."

Cameron studied them both. *They didn't get it, did they?* Not even Morgan could understand what was happening inside of him. The wolf was looking out for him, protecting his life, but increasingly it felt like it had a mind of its own.

He let out a frustrated breath, and pushed the thought away. *Deal with the problem at hand, Cam.*

He flipped the lid on Montmorency's laptop. "Mad isn't it? I've been hanging about the Parallel so long, if someone says 'web' I think Weaver Daemon..."

"Makes sense," said Morgan. "They're sneaky. You've gotta watch out for them."

"That's not what I meant. The point's this: we've been chasing Grey, but *Black's* involved too. That means we have to investigate in the Human World as well. Black's human, so he must have a trail online. Everyone does."

"The 'great Dr Alasdair Black'. That's what Grey called him." Eve clapped her hands. "We can look him up!"

"Way ahead of you." Cameron beckoned Eve and Morgan to cluster round the screen. "I found Black's University profile page. Look."

There was a black-and-white headshot of Dr Black looking poised and determined, and below it a list of the classes he taught and his publications and research interests.

"So he's a physicist," said Eve. "*That* sort of doctor. Studying 'dark matter and the structure of the material universe'." She pulled a face. "Fascinating. But what does it mean?"

"I googled. Dark matter is something to do with the hidden mass of the universe. Scientists reckon there's not enough stars and planets and stuff to balance everything out, and explain how gravity really works... I didn't entirely understand. But I got to looking down his list of sources for his current project, and something leapt out."

Eve read the block of text that Cameron high-lighted.

"'On the True Nature of this Human Sphere, and its Maleficent Daemonic Counterweight': an unpublished codex by Alexander Mitchell, retrieved from private collection."

"Mitchell was one of the World Split dudes," said Morgan, "along with the daemon-mage, Astredo. It was them that tried to push the Human and Daemon worlds apart, so there'd be no more crossovers – and accidentally created the Parallel instead." He gave an amused grunt. "Boom! Big accident."

"You amaze me. You *know* things." Eve flared her eyes in mock surprise. "I mean, I knew that, but so do you..."

"Course I do." Morgan glared. "Everyone on the Parallel does. It's basic."

141

Cameron nodded. "It's one of the first things Gran taught me. She said how vastly, madly dangerous the magic was as well. The place Mitchell worked his magic rite, up on Arthur's Seat, is still a source of power." He shut his eyes for a second. "That's why she took me there, on the anniversary of the World Split. To try and use that power..." He tailed off, remembering things he'd prefer not to.

"And the power took her away," said Morgan gently, "but you came back stronger. Wolfier!"

"Something like that."

"Hold on." Eve waved her hands in an agitated fashion. "Watt was fixing a machine called a 'World Engine'. He was going to use it on the Parallel... What if that's Black and Grey's plan? What if they want to finish what Mitchell and Astredo started, all those years ago?" She leapt to her feet. "They empty the Parallel, run the Engine – and totally separate the Human and Daemon worlds!"

Morgan whistled. "Black's just about mad enough to do it."

"And they're clearing out the Parallel so they can get started," added Eve.

"Turning it back into the void between worlds it originally was," said Cameron. "World Split v 2.0." Suddenly, his face contorted and he clutched at his head and cried out.

"Cam! Are you ok?" Eve's voice filled with concern.

"It's the wolf – the wolf again. He *really* doesn't like it when the Parallel's threatened. Doesn't like it at all."

"I'll get you some water." Eve started to move to the kitchen.

"Mate, you've got to stop talking about 'the wolf' like that," said Morgan urgently. "It makes no sense. It's just *you* –"

"Oh, leave him alone," Eve shot back over her shoulder. "Can't you see he's not feeling well? I'll see if I can find an aspirin –" She stopped short and gasped. "*The lump! It's broken out!*"

Both boys leapt to their feet and ran for the back of the shop. The lump had swollen grotesquely, cracking the dish that confined it. Fragments of china dotted its puffball skin while four wooden legs protruded at odd angles out the bottom.

"It got out the other way: eating through the base," Morgan shouted. "Cunning little..."

Eve tried to edge past the quivering mass. The remaining table stumps were swiftly drawn in. The blob *glooped*, growing in size, and rolling like a monstrous tumbleweed to block her off. She turned and darted the other way, but again it followed, stretching out its grey dough consistency until it spread at waist-height across the width of the store.

"It's no use – I can't get round it!"

"Can you jump?" Cameron encouraged her.

A mouth with chalky teeth puckered open. "Excellent suggestion, sir. This lump has dined too long on table. I hunger for something with a bit more fight."

Cameron roared. He grabbed instrument after

dusty instrument from the wall pegboards and shelves and threw them at the lump. A trumpet, piano accordion, and banjo were swiftly and noisily swallowed.

The lump gurgled contentedly and continued to swell. Morgan grabbed Cameron's arm. "It's no good. You're feeding it – just making it stronger."

"You got a better idea? What else can I do?"

Eve pointed to the kitchen door, and the spiral stair beyond. "I'm going down – it's my only chance."

"No!" Cameron yelled. "There's no way out. It's a dead end!"

"I've got to risk it! There's the steel door over the sub-basement. Maybe that'll stop it!" She turned and ran for the kitchen as the pulsing, growing grey blob rolled after her.

CHAPTER 12

CHASE TO CALTON HILL

The grey mass pushed against the bowed window of the shop. As Cameron watched, the panes began to buckle and crack. There was nothing they could do to stop the lump's progress. He and Morgan had been beaten back; forced out onto the outside stairs that led up to pavement level. Montmorency's netbook – still displaying Dr Black's hawk-like features – was all he'd managed to salvage.

"Woah! How did it get so big?" said Morgan. "Where does it all come from?"

"The other blobs must've done their work, so he's got energy to spare..." Cameron shot a savage glance at Morgan. "You know what? I'm not interested how the Amazing Expanding Man does his tricks. All I know is he's got Eve, and there's nothing I can do." He slammed the railings, which thrummed in protest.

"She'll be ok. That's a big old door down there."

Shards of glass clinked as another pane popped. Metres away on the street, people were walking about but none of them reacted. They just kept their heads down and moved on.

"Hey! Does nobody want to help?" Cameron shouted. "My friend's about to be swallowed by a huge fungus monster, and no one cares."

A schoolgirl pushed her headphones deeper into her ears, and an old man became very interested in his phone.

"Sheep! That's what you lot are. Dumb sheep. Baa! BAAAA!"

"Mate, remember where you are, eh?" Morgan wrapped his arms round Cameron's chest and dragged him back down the shop's stairs. He hissed urgently in his friend's ear. "If you're gonna wolf out, the middle of the Human city is the worst place to do it. Those dafties might zone out on something grey and stinky glooping against a basement window, but a full-on boy-to-wolf transformation? Not so much! *Now get a hold of yourself!*"

"Get off! I'm not gonna shift!" Cameron struggled.

"How do you know? Because right now your control is kind of lacking –"

"I just do! My head..." Cameron frowned and suddenly went still. "It's gone quiet. It's not howling anymore..."

"Then you're calming down. That's a good sign."

"I don't know. It's different." Cameron's brow furrowed. "Morgan, I can't sense it at all..."

146

"I'd like a hug too, if there's one going," said an amused voice from above them.

"Eve!"

The two boys broke apart and Cameron bounded up the stairs to embrace Eve. "You're all right. I thought it had got you!"

"Not this time." Eve smiled and then gave Morgan a quick hug as well. She was looking more than a little bedraggled, her clothes streaked with dirt and powdery dust threaded through her black hair. "Turns out there's a hidden passageway. It's pretty dank and crumbly, and comes out in the back garden of a tenement round the corner. I had to climb over a wall to get out."

Morgan scratched his chin. "I've scoped that basement properly. There's no exit."

Eve shook her head. "I don't know if it's leftover from Janus's portal magic, or if Cam's sneaky gran had it built it as an escape route, but it's definitely there. He showed me."

"Who are you talking about?"

She raised her hand and pointed.

Pressed against the side of a building, out of the yellow glare of the street lamps, lurked the silhouette of a wolf.

Morgan thrust his chin forward and sniffed the air. "I must be going mad, but that's…"

"You're not," Eve said quietly. "I felt that too. That's why I trusted him."

The shape moved and raised its snout. Brilliant green eyes flared, looking first to Eve, then Morgan and finally to Cameron.

A shudder ran through him – a queasy ripple that was part alarm and part recognition. The only thing he could compare it to was stumbling to the bathroom in the middle of the night and catching a glimpse of a sleep-blurred face in the mirror and, just for a second, not knowing it was your own.

"Cameron, he looks just like the Other You," said Eve.

Cameron moved toward the black furred shape. It seemed to be more shadow than wolf. In response it turned and darted away, quick as a thought.

"We've got to follow him," said Cameron.

"Oh great. Must we?" Eve groaned and pulled cobwebs from her hair. "Because I've already had a trying day –"

But Cameron had started running, and Morgan was close behind.

Cameron powered through the streets. The wolf seemed to flicker as it ran, gaining solidity then fading back into night. There were moments when the track went cold, then he would catch a flash of green eyes – and that sudden stab of recognition. Contact re-established, the wolf would turn and run once more.

The crowds thickened as he neared the top of Leith Walk. The wolf raced across the busy road, weaving through four lanes of traffic.

A car slammed on its brakes.

"Control your dog!" someone shouted.

"Love to," Cameron threw over his shoulder, and pressed on.

The wolf disappeared down a steep road by the side of the Playhouse Theatre. At the bottom, a neglected courtyard gave onto a drying green with bins and lines of frosted washing.

"Where's he gone?" Eve searched, black hair flying out behind her.

"It's ok, I've got the scent." Morgan's head was held high. "Nose is never wrong." There was a hint of a movement at the corner of the green. "*There!*"

Cameron pounded onwards, trainers scrunching on cold gravel, following a winding path that led past an old church and up the side of Calton Hill. His heart thumped as the gradient increased, the wolf ahead loping between patches of darkness. All at once, the path levelled out. The city was revealed spread below them: all grey stone and bristling with wintery light.

"Lost him. Gah!" Morgan skidded to a halt and spat in disgust.

"So much for Super Nose." Eve bent over, breathing heavily.

"He can't have just vanished!"

"Why not? Ghost Wolf just *appeared*, after all."

"Scent is *historic*, right? I can track across time as well as place. Even if he'd shifted to the Parallel there'd be something left behind." Morgan rubbed the back of his neck. "Must've gone somewhere I can't track."

"Back to where he came from?" Eve huffed out

chilly air and turned to Cameron. "Wherever that was. What do you reckon?"

"Not sure... I just knew he wanted me to follow him." Cameron looked vague for a second. He rubbed the side of his head. "I think we're here for a reason."

Morgan exchanged glances with Eve. "Ok, mate. You're in charge, because I haven't got a clue right now. Where next?"

Cameron scanned his surroundings. The hilltop was a strange cold place, scattered with statues and old buildings. There was a tower shaped like an up-turned telescope, a huge domed monument sheltering an urn, and a green-roofed observatory. Further away, on a flattish plain, a row of giant stone columns was lit up against the night sky. Arranged around three sides of an otherwise empty space, they gave the startling impression someone had randomly dropped half a Greek temple onto the hill.

At the base of the columns, a group of men in tattered bird costumes seemed to be practising some sort of play. They moved back and forth in a ritualised dance, the feathers on their clothes fluttering in the wind.

After a year living in Edinburgh, Cameron was used to seeing performers in unusual outfits wandering the streets, promoting their shows. But this was months before the Festival started.

He beckoned his friends and pointed. "I've got a feeling we should start over there."

They made their way across the grass. As they approached the performers, one of them broke away, walking with a stiff-legged gait. Shiny black and white feathers were stitched into the weave of his business suit and the top of his bowler hat. His face was lacquered with greasepaint and a pointed cardboard beak had been tied around his head with string.

"Looks like a magpie," Eve said tentatively. "Is that what you are?"

The performer's head jerked back in indignation. His gloved hand indicated the full length of his body from clawed boot to beak. His chest puffed out. He made no sound, but the meaning of his dumb show was obvious: Meant to be a magpie? I *am* a magpie.

"Ok, Magpie-Banker," said Eve. "Maybe you can help. We're looking for a wolf."

The bird-man blinked for a second. He pointed at Morgan then Cameron and cocked his head. He covered his mouth and shook convulsively.

"The four-legged kind," Morgan growled. "You bird-brained –"

"Morgan! Be nice. I'm sure Mr Magpie would help if he could. Perhaps if we traded something?" Eve reached to her wrist and unclasped a shiny bracelet. She dangled it in the air. "Bet you'd like this?"

The performer opened his mouth and let loose a deafening, rattling squawk right in Eve's face. Startled, she dropped the bracelet. He snatched it and strutted away.

"Now hold on..." Morgan was instantly on the warpath. His chest swelled belligerently and he stalked after the thief.

The magpie-man's eyes went wide. He gestured towards the three-sided monument and squawked again. His hand foraged inside his suit and he produced a business card, which he handed to Eve with a flourish. The typewritten message said:

Come to the Augury
Diverse Questions Answered
via
The Medium of Birds

AAARK!

"I've heard of the Augur of Calton Hill," said Cameron. "Gran told me about him once. It's how she discovered where to go for her resurrection magic."

The bird-man made a rolling gesture with his glove. Eve turned the card and read the reverse. In smaller type it said:

Terms and Conditions Apply:
1. The Augur will Answer <u>Strictly</u> the First Question put to Him.
2. Only One Question per Applicant.
3. Entry is by Ordeal - You Shall Confront That Which you Fear the Most.

And then, in a smaller font still:

The Calton Hill Auguries accept no liability for death, disaster or insanity experienced by applicants.
Let Courage be your Watchword & Knowledge your True Reward!

Eve sighed. "Oh brilliant. Why couldn't it be an ordeal by hot chocolate? Or puppies?"

"It augurs well for your future," Morgan said slowly. Cameron and Eve looked at him. "That two-faced god must've known we'd come here... That's what he said when he gave us the Omniclavis. It got stuck inside my head."

"Where it no doubt had loads of space to roam about freely," Eve said brightly. She bit her lip. "Sorry, I joke when I'm nervous. Haven't you noticed?"

"We don't have to go," said Cameron, watching her with concern. "They can't make us. We can head back down the hill and go home –"

"To the shop filled with Grey, or the house with no wards? Great options, mate. And with the Parallel shutting up, my favourite bolt-holes are all out of commission."

"Morgan –" said Cameron warningly.

"No, he's right," said Eve. "We've got *loads* of questions, like how do we beat Grey and Black, and stop them destroying the Parallel? And what's up with you changing into a wolf all the time?" She took a deep breath. "We've got to go through with it."

"Ordeal of fear it is, then." Cameron gave a determined grin. "Let's world-shift and get on with it." He closed his eyes and let the song of the Parallel wash over him.

On the hillside, the monument began to grow. Pillar after pillar sprouted, rising up from the earth like colossal stone palm trees. Laurel-decorated lintels faded into being, joining together with the building's fast-emerging fourth side. The newly formed quadrangle was open to the sky and every surface teemed with avian life. On the ground, small birds like starlings, pigeons and robins congregated, while high on the tops of the columns owls hooted, gulls screeched and sharp-beaked raptors scanned for prey with robotic precision.

As the Parallel settled and stabilised, Cameron once more heard the low call of a wolf – so close it was as if a whiskery muzzle was pressed tight to his face, a cold nose touching his cheek. This time he had no doubt where the howl was coming from: the wolf presence that had vanished earlier had returned.

So you're back with me, are you? he whispered, feeling strangely reassured. *Good. Let's see what trouble you've got us into.*

Morgan was studying the many-pillared monument. He whistled. "Bit squawky now it's gone auto-complete, but standing strong. You've got to respect that. No Greys here!"

"No," said Cameron. "Not yet."

The magpie-daemon had transformed too, becoming more bird than costumed man. His feathers protruded directly from his skin, their lustrous sheen glinting in the torchlight that burned at the corners of the Parthenon-style temple. He clacked his beak. "Travellers three, if you wish to enter the Augur's cave, you must show me some *spine.*"

"Yeah, yeah." Morgan gave him a baleful look.

"Trial by fear. We get it. When do we start?"

The magpie-daemon chittered and jabbed at Morgan.

"Hey, what's that for?" Morgan took a step backwards, raising an arm to protect his face. No longer tawdry painted cardboard, the daemon's bill was razor sharp.

Another bird-man left the group that had been dancing together. His feathers were thick and white, his eyes disturbingly large and gold. "Make a pen to unlock a mind," it cawed at Cameron, "from a tool of flight left behind – what is it?"

"How do you mean?"

The owl-daemon hooted, and swiped at him. Cameron yelped and ducked.

"There's more coming." Eve pointed. "Look out!"

Obsidian-black crows the size of burly wrestlers strutted forward, chanting, "Sturdy stem and jagged edge, often lost behind the hedge; collect a set, put 'em by; pick the one that lets you fly."

"It's a riddle!" shouted Cameron. As the yammering, chattering crowd of bird-daemons clustered closer, pushing and shoving, he tried to remember everything that had been said. *Spine... lost behind the hedge...a tool of flight that could be made into a pen... a quill!* "Feathers! They're all descriptions of feathers!"

"And?" a gull-daemon cawed. "And? And? And?"

"You want *more*?"

"Something that allows flight... escape... with stem and jagged edge." Eve's eyes lit up. "They're talking about *keys* as well!"

The screeching frenzy of the bird-men slowed, but they continued to jab and jostle. "And? And? And?"

"We're not there yet," Cameron jumped up, trying to see Morgan and Eve over the scrum. "What can be a feather *and* a key? Gah! I hate cryptic crosswords. And you can just shove off." He pushed at a long-legged heron-daemon. "Come on! When is a feather a key – or a key like a feather?"

"When it's a mighty morphing super-key!" Morgan roared, tearing the Omniclavis out from round his neck. "Come on, you pecking horrors, see what you make of this!"

He held the Omniclavis aloft. It grew long and thin, its jagged metal tines becoming down-soft. For a moment, the outline of a feather was superimposed on top, then it blew up and into the air, leaving Morgan clutching just the ordinary key-shaped Omniclavis again.

The crowd of bird daemons froze.

"Strike two," Cameron observed. "One left!"

"Still no sparkles." Eve pulled herself out from under the wing of a greasy pigeon-daemon.

They watched as the feather blew over the monument. A *skraarking* cry echoed and three tall spaces in between the columns abruptly grew dark, the hillside beyond vanishing from view.

"Access to the Augury!" Cameron punched the air. "We did it!"

"Personally I'm impressed by my deductive brilliance," said Morgan.

"*Our* deductive brilliance –" Cameron began, then

156

he let loose an involuntary cry as a set of nail-sharp talons gripped him from behind, and pointed feet kicked his shins. He was being frogmarched towards the space between two pillars. To either side of him, crow-daemons were propelling a struggling Eve and Morgan forward as well.

"This'll be the test!" he yelled. "Quick! We've got to decide what we're asking. We can't all say the same thing. Each choose a question, and *stick to it*, whatever happens."

"The Greys. I wanna know how to get 'em. I'll ask how to stop the Greys." Morgan twisted sharply in the bird-man's grip, tearing free. "Leave off, crow-breath! If I'm going in, it's under my own power. See you on the other side!" With a raucous whoop, he ran towards the opening and vanished.

"Eve! What about you?"

"Dr Black," Eve gasped. "I'll find out how to stop Dr Black. He's the smart one." Her face contorted as she neared the portal between the pillars "Cameron, I really am scared..."

"Don't be. You'll be great!"

"But it's my greatest fear, Cam. *I know what that is!* I can't –"

Her voice cut off abruptly.

"Guess it's up to me to ask how to save the Parallel..." A claw shoved in Cameron's back and he toppled headfirst through the opening. There was the sound of a thousand bird wings flapping, and everything went dark.

CHAPTER 13

WEREWOLF PARALLEL

AAAAAAAAAAAAAAAAAARRK!

Cameron reached out and slammed down his palm, muffling the awful cry. A moment passed as he came properly to his senses, then he drew the hand holding his phone back under the covers and cancelled the hated alarm.

6.55 AM

Did he really have to get up? Already?

Yes. Yes, he did — if he was to stand any chance of making it down the road, onto the bus and across town in time for his shift at Odyssey.

As he soaped his hair in the shower — choosing to set the grubby dial to Too Hot (not Ice Cold) — an ooky sensation churned in his stomach. It was like there was something stressing him, something important he'd forgotten to do...

158

...some trial or ordeal he had to face up to...

Rent was due next week, and there was his share of the bills as well, but he'd have just enough to cover that, if he was careful... His horrible boss would tear a strip off him if he was late – he was always looking for an excuse to change Cameron, to squash him down and reshape him into someone more punctual and efficient – but that wasn't any different to usual either... It was just another ordinary, boring day.

Like any other.

In the kitchen, Eve sat at the formica table, reading the *Cauldlockheart Courier*. She was staring at a 'Whatever happened to...?' article about people who'd been on talent shows on the telly.

"You remember Rhys Wright?" she said, not looking up.

"Vaguely." Cameron hastily buttered some toast. "He was the one that looked like a duck, right?"

"I thought he was cute." Eve pouted. "Anyway, he's been chucked off that soap opera, *Prophecies*. The producers think no one's interested in him any more. He's back living with his mum, and stacking shelves in a supermarket. It's terrible."

"Eve," he said. "You stack shelves. I stack shelves. It's what people do."

"Yeah, but it's not like we've ever done anything different, is it?" She put her coffee mug down on Rhys Wright's beaming duck-face. "Imagine having all that, and then going back to being normal."

159

"Shocking." Cameron brushed some crumbs off his work baseball cap. "At least he got a chance to try something else."

How had he ended up flat-sharing with Eve again?

He remembered she'd been staying in some grim spider-infested place in a posh street in Edinburgh, but it all seemed a bit vague...

"See you later, eh?"

"Mmmm." Eve flipped the page, the story forgotten. She lifted her hand and made an approximation of a tipping motion. "Maybe at Black's, yeah?"

"I guess. Not like there's anywhere else, is there?"

Outside it was a nothing-sort-of day, the sky flat and white like someone had forgotten to add the colour. Seemed ages since he'd seen any different... The queasy sensation plucked at him again as he neared Odyssey. He pulled his greasy baseball cap straight on his head. He had to be wearing it in sight of the store, or Mr Grey would have a fit.

His boss was a stickler like that.

The front of the shop was bright and gleaming — all fresh carpets, scented plastic and glowing computer screens. The customers would come in, browse for their choice among thousands of goods, and order it up. A few minutes later, their shiny new microwave or hamster cage or set of earrings or whatever would come trundling down a conveyer belt — as if by magic — to be handed over by the smiling counter staff.

"There's no magic of course. Just sweat and hard graft," Mr Grey had said to Cameron on his first day, as he led him to the cavernous warehouse behind the scenes. "You backroom elves simply keep an eye on the display, and when a code number pops up, you go bounding off and find the product." Grey massaged his chin and eyed Cameron doubtfully. "The first letter and number combination gives you the row, the second the aisle, and finally the appropriate bay. Do you think you can manage that?"

"Of course. I'm not stupid."

"I hope not. Your CV was hardly sparkling. No qualifications at all, tut, tut. How do you account for that?"

Cameron gave his new boss his blankest look. He'd long since grown tired of explaining his circumstances. "My dad died. I ended up living with my gran, working for her. She didn't care if I went back to school at all, so I never did. She went a bit mad in the end."

"And now you're on your own, trying to make it in the big bad world." Grey placed a clammy hand on Cameron's shoulder. His breath was awful, somehow sugary and mushroomy all at once, and Cameron fought the urge to choke.

"Something like that."

"Commendable to see you facing up to your responsibilities. Stick with me, young sir, and good things will happen. Work hard! Don't ask questions. In no time at all, you shall have a promotion. The Odyssey won't be a single store forever." Grey's face contorted into a ghastly leer. "I have such plans for expansion..."

That had been three years ago.

Three years that had passed in a blur of squeaking conveyer belts, and the hefting and carrying of endless boxes and parcels.

Same old, same old, thought Cameron.

But part of him thought it wasn't 'same old' at all.

He felt sometimes there was some other place he should be, something else he should be doing, but what? These feelings weren't exactly new. He'd had them almost as long as he could remember. He'd never entirely fitted in... not back at school, not in his second home with his cold grandma, and certainly not in the Odyssey warehouse.

And what happened to people who didn't fit in?

"You can't change the world, so you must change yourself," Mr Grey said whenever he caught Cameron daydreaming. "Learn to conform — or go under."

"Yes, Mr Grey," Cameron would say automatically. He didn't see any alternative.

Today, as he clocked-on, he saw Grey was giving his usual dreary welcoming speech to a new recruit: a stocky older boy with messy fair hair. The boy had a look of utter boredom on his face. He caught

Cameron's eye and yawned massively, exposing surprisingly sharp teeth.

Cameron looked away, fearing trouble, but Grey didn't seem to notice. He gestured at the recruit's scruffy biker boots, "Those are non-regulation, and as for the hair..." His chins shook with disapproval. "Keep it contained, or better still, get it cut. Otherwise there will be no hope for you."

As Grey retreated to his office, the boy plucked off his cap and stuck his fingers up in a rude gesture behind Grey's back.

"You don't want to do that," Cameron murmured. "Grey's got cameras hidden everywhere. He's always scanning the recordings."

The boy shrugged. "Like I care. I'm not going to be here long. I got plans."

"I had those once. When I was younger."

The boy arched an eyebrow. "You're not exactly ancient." He thrust out a hand. "I'm —"

An image of a white wolf, running through the night, and a name. Mo—

"—Morgan, by the way. How long have you been in hell?"

"Cameron. And about three years."

Morgan adopted an incredulous expression. "How do you stand it?"

Cameron shrugged. "Don't have much choice." He gestured to the single big LCD screen that hung over them like a watchful eye. "Come on, store's open. That's the first order coming up. I'll better show you how this works."

They moved down the dingy aisles. Morgan lifted his nose and sniffed. "It's kind of damp in here. Mouldy."

"That's why the stuff's all wrapped up in plastic. But everything Grey sells stinks a bit."

"So old Grey sells shonky goods. You amaze me."

"Every Odyssey needs a monster. At least he's not a flesh-eating cyclops."

"Huh?"

"The *Odyssey.* The store's named after an ancient story by Homer. It's an epic quest with giants and sirens and killer whirlpools and all sorts."

The boy threw him a calculating look. "You're smart. Why are you here, exactly?"

"Didn't get the grades. Long story. What's your excuse?"

"Need some money. But it's just work. I'm more about the sounds." Morgan gave a lop-sided grin. "I'm in a band."

"Oh yeah?" Cameron tried to keep the flicker of jealousy out his voice. There'd been a time, not so very long ago really, when he'd get ideas for songs running through his head. He'd wanted to be in a band more than anything else in the world. It had been all he dreamed about and —

music could open up another world to him, but —

he didn't have much time for that now.

"What's your band called?"

"The Pack. Or Full Moon." Morgan looked sheepish. "We keep changing. Lately it's Wolf Month... Or Werewolf Parallel."

"I like Wolf Month. Short and punchy."

"Yeah, me too. But the guys think it's too subtle. People won't get it." Morgan pulled a face. He thumbed a photocopied sign tacked to the end of a row of stacking cabinets. "Down here, right?"

"Yup," said Cameron absently, thinking of Morgan's band. "So you're into the whole werewolf thing, then? Do you go on stage all big sideburns, quiffs and pointy teeth?"

"Well obviously. Because that wouldn't be at all lame." Morgan slanted a glance at him. "The name's more about what the music does to you when you're playing, and really feeling it, you know?"

Cameron remembered what that had been like. Just losing yourself in sound...

"Not really," he lied.

"Oh man, it's the best. Sets free the real you — the one you usually have to hide inside..." Morgan stopped dead in his tracks. "J7 P10 X12."

"What?"

"This is the aisle, dafty." He peered up the teetering stacks into the darkness. "Looks like it's all the way up."

"It's ok. I'll get a ladder." That queasy feeling was rising in Cameron's guts again — the nagging

165

sense there was something hugely important he was forgetting or missing out on. He pushed the thought away, found the nearest set of metal steps and rolled them along to the required bay.

"I used to play guitar a bit," he ventured. "Just acoustic. I never got an amp,"

Morgan started to climb. "What happened?"

"Gave it up. Too much effort. Takes practice and time." He shrugged. "I wasn't any good really."

"Oh... Bet you are."

Cameron laughed. "Oh yeah? How do you know? You've never heard me play a note."

"Just a feeling. I saw that look in your eye when I was talking. Like you wanted to be in The Pack —"

"Or Werewolf Parallels or whatever you're calling yourselves today —"

"Why not? If that's what you want."

Cameron blushed and said nothing.

"You'd need to be free at night. We're just starting to get gigs, maybe one a month. We're playing this evening at The Alhambra. It's a converted cinema, but of a dump, but —" Morgan paused and whooped. "Oh no way. I know what J7 P10 X12 is." He clattered back down the steel steps holding a guitar-shaped bundle. "It's an acoustic! Like you used to play. What say we cut it open, and you show me what you can do?"

"You mean — an audition?"

"Sure!"

Cameron's heart was pounding. There was

something about the guitar in its plastic cocoon that made him feel as if he was standing on the edge of a cliff and daring himself to leap off. "Nah, we'd get in trouble with Grey. He'd kill us."

Morgan made a dismissive noise. He ferreted in his pocket and produced a brass key. "Here. I'll get it open —"

An impossible two-faced man held out a key. "Now pay attention, wolf-boys; three times only the Omniclavis will work —"

"There should be sparkles," Cameron said.

"You what?"

"Something a friend of mine says. Here, don't mess up your door key." He dug in his trouser pocket and drew out a penknife he used for cutting packaging. A strange thrill ran through him as he held the knife, poised to slice the wrapping open. "I'm not sure we should be doing this."

"Live a little." The boy grinned wolfishly. "It'll be worth it to have that music running through your veins again, going wild —"

"Mr Morgan, you are dismissed." Grey's voice thundered out of the warehouse's PA system and Cameron's knife clattered to the floor. "Security has been called and are on their way."

There was the rhythmic stomp of heavy boots on concrete floors. Guards were approaching from either end of the long aisle. To Cameron's mind, they resembled squatter, uglier clones of Grey. *There was something freakish about that — the way his heavies looked just like him...*

"You will be escorted from the building," Grey's amplified voice announced.

"Not flaming likely." Morgan started to hurl boxes from the lower racks, creating an escape tunnel to the next aisle through the back of the open shelving. "Come on, what are you waiting for?"

"I can't." Cameron held back, watching. "This is it. This is my job. I can't just go running away with some mad grunger."

"Your call, mate. I'm not hanging around to be thrown out. Wouldn't give them the satisfaction." Morgan flung himself into the gap, and began to wriggle through dextrously. "Remember, we're playing The Alhambra tonight, if you change your mind."

He dropped to the ground on the other side with a thump. The grim-faced guards spun on their respective heels, and began remorselessly to retrace their steps.

"And what of you, Cameron Duffy?" Grey's voice boomed. "Will you follow your ruffian friend?"

"No." Cameron looked down at his trainers. "I can't."

Grey laughed. "I see my trust in you was not misplaced. Why, with a few more years' toil, I might consider moving you upwards. And if you keep going — and really apply yourself — one day you could be just like me. Another Mr Grey! How would you like that?"

"Just like you?" Cameron felt sick.

"Oh yes. I have a way of spotting talent, of *absorbing* the best... In the end, I always get what I want."

A grey puffball grew and grew, drawing in the instruments that they desperately flung at it, forcing them back and out into the street, –

"I could *never* be like you," Cameron shouted. He snatched up the discarded guitar, and ripped open its wrapping. Memories were flooding through him, of songs and freedom and music, of the person he was really meant to be. "This feeling I have that I don't fit in... Maybe that *doesn't* mean there's something wrong with me. Maybe it just means I was meant to find somewhere better."

Grey's disembodied voice raged from the speakers. "I warn you, boy; if you touch that you will pay for it. You will never stop paying for it!"

Cameron ignored him. A tune was forming in his head, a song with a rocking, strolling rhythm that spoke to him of somewhere else, far away from his dull life here – a place filled with danger and monsters and excitement.

Maybe Morgan would let him play it at the Alhambra, with Werewolf Parallel...

His fingers formed a pattern on the fretboard. He lifted his other hand to strum the strings – and with that chord, the whole world changed...

CHAPTER 14

THE WOLF IS WOKEN

"A good choice, playing the guitar."

Cameron was sitting on a pile of skins at the back of a draughty cave, his hands clutching at midair. An old man with tufted white hair and intense blue eyes was watching him with an expression of wry amusement.

"Personally I favour the fiddle, but still..."

Cameron's arms dropped to his sides. He opened his mouth but the old man lifted a bony finger and made a sibilant shushing sound. "Don't go saying anything daft like 'where am I?' or 'what's going on?' or 'what sort of fur is this, because it's awffy cosy?' Those would count as *first questions* and that's what I'm bound to answer. You'd be amazed how many folks waste their chance. You may only go through the ordeal once."

"The warehouse... Eve and Morgan and the guitar,"

said Cameron, as the meaning of the old man's speech sunk in. "That was the tes—"

"For your sake, laddie, I'm going to assume that was a statement, not a question. Your last warning, mark you!" The old man grinned impishly, baring his few remaining teeth. "That was the test, yes, and I am Cutler, also known as the Augur of Calton Hill."

Cameron rubbed his eyes, fighting the impulse to ask how long he'd been imagining his other life. "It felt real, like I'd been there forever."

"It was an ordeal, laddie. What were you expecting? High Tea with jam and scones?"

"No, but —"

"That comes after." Cutler hobbled to a low table. "Well, it would if I had any. I have to rely on what my birds can forage." He returned with a broken oatcake and a glass of something brown and brackish.

"It'll do ye good," he admonished, observing Cameron's sceptical expression. "Now tell me, laddie – and never mind the year, because at my age they're all much the same, just a wee bit chillier or warmer – what's the date in the Human World outside?"

"January 27th, I think," said Cameron through a mouthful of stale oatcake. "Or it was when I came here."

"Aye, that would figure. You're deep in the wolf month now. That's what they called it, when the cold is at its worst, and things grow desperate and dark, and you face the greatest chance of being consumed by a wolf…" The old man looked at Cameron shrewdly.

"That holds true for the wolf inside too. Now ask your question."

"I passed the..." Cameron bit his tongue and swiftly re-arranged his words. "I get a question, *because* I passed the test. That was definitely a statement, by the way."

"Well caught," said Cutler. "Yes. You faced your greatest fear."

"So my fear is," Cameron fought to keep all hint of questioning incredulity out his voice, "I end up working in a catalogue store."

"No. You fear that you will lose all that makes you different, become an ordinary human again, and so be forced to return to the world you left behind."

"Oh." Cameron considered the Augur's words – and realised their truth.

Since his dad had died, he'd been thrown into a Parallel realm of mayhem and magic that was dangerous, but kind of wonderful as well. For the past year, running wild on wolf nights and taking over his gran's old business with Eve and Morgan, he'd felt like he'd found his place at last. He had no wish to go back to his previous life at all. *What was there for him now?* Only his school friend Amy, and although he liked and cared for her, sometimes she reminded him a little too much of his old problems. The Augur's ordeal – although it had been surreal and dreamlike – had also been the closest he had come to 'real life' in quite some time...

"To be fair," Cameron said, "that *is* pretty scary."

"Still... you triumphed. You gave them what for."

"But all I did was pick up a guitar! It wasn't anything special."

"It was enough. The choice revealed your true nature." The Augur's finger prodded Cameron's forehead. "Music runs through you as strongly as the wolf does, and it may outlast it – if the wolf has other plans."

"Other plans!" Cameron swallowed. "That's mad. You're talking like it's a separate thing. The wolf is me. It's just me. It's me when I change."

"That was how it began, but that's not all it is now." The Augur's eyes glittered. "Your Were-side comes not only from the wolf-boy who saved your life, but from the Parallel itself." He waved his wrinkled claw of a hand. *"Remember..."*

A vision leapt into Cameron's mind, of that last night on Arthur's Seat with his treacherous grandmother.

She'd opened a portal that led to the ancient heart of the Parallel. As the power coursed, he had grown weaker and she had grown stronger. Morgan had prowled and raged in wolf-form, unable to help, until at last a desperate solution presented itself.

"No, Morgan, not her! Bite me, bite me!"

"The Parallel was part of the wolf's birth, and its claim is very strong indeed. It has gifted you a champion. Why do you think your powers exceed that of other Weres?"

"No." Cameron's brow knitted. He didn't want

to hear this. "The shifts happen when I need them, that's all. Like he's watching out for me –"

"And who would 'he' be?"

"The wolf inside, of course. The other me..." Cameron tailed off.

The Augur nodded. "You've already sensed it. The wolf has woken. He knows who he must protect, and who he must fight. He has already started to slip free, and run by himself."

"That's not true! It can't be."

"He led you to me, did he not? You followed his shadow, all the way to Calton Hill, after he saved your friend."

The stab of recognition that accompanied his every glance at the wolf... It wasn't just Cameron who'd thought it was familiar – Morgan had tracked the wolf's scent and Eve had known him too. Cameron had felt its presence leave his mind when Eve was in danger, and return as he had world-shifted through to the Parallel, up by the monument on Calton Hill.

He had to face it. *The wolf was him – but it wasn't him as well.* Somehow his wolf-side was getting out of control.

"What's going to happen to me?" he blurted – and clapped his hand over his mouth. "No, that's not it! That's not my question! I take it back!"

"You cannot. It's been asked."

The Augur turned and shuffled towards the mouth of the cave. Cameron hurried after, pulling himself up sharp as he realised the opening gave onto a sheer drop. Beneath a glowering dark green sky lay the Parallel version of the city: its teetering towers, domes and tenements a twisted, higgledy-piggeldy reflection of its Human World counterpart. He had never seen the Parallel from such a vantage point before, but any pleasure he might have felt was short-lived. A familiar low wolfish moan sounded in his ear as he realised, one by one, the city's lights were fading out.

"The Greys approach," said Cutler. "Daemonkind are fleeing the Parallel for the safety of their own world. Soon even the Augury will be under threat."

"That makes it worse." Cameron rubbed at his chest with his fist. "I meant to ask how to save the Parallel. That's what I planned. I've let everyone down."

It was all going to come true: the strange, bleak, magic-free existence he'd inhabited in his ordeal. Grey would empty the Parallel, Dr Black and Watt would run their Engine, and the worlds would be torn apart forever...

"Dinna fret, laddie." The Augur patted vaguely at his arm. "What you asked and what you meant to ask may be closer than you think. My birds will know the truth of it."

He cast his arms wide, muttering under his breath. There was the sound of beating wings, and the light filtering into the cave cut out. The rush of feathery motion passed, and Cameron's eyes widened as he took in what was happening.

Hundreds of birds were rising from the trees, rooftops, nooks and crannies of the city, surging past the cave and soaring upwards in billowing plumes. For a moment, the black lines coalesced against the sky, and seemed to outline the face of a wolf. Then the pattern was broken.

"I've not seen this before. The fates are too finely balanced." The Augur raised his arms further, the material of his monk's habit hanging down like wings. In response, the birds rose again, spiralling faster and faster. No outline emerged this time – the pattern remained chaotic. As Cameron watched, some of the distant black dots started to rocket into each other and spiral downwards.

"They're falling," he said. "Falling out the sky."

The Augur's face rumpled. "The wolf will save you or destroy you, that's all I can see. Perhaps it will be both all at once."

"That's no use! How can it be both?" Cameron yelled, barely containing the urge to shake the old man. "Which is it? Which'll it be?"

Cutler's eyes blazed, suddenly yellow-bright and owl-like. "You will only win by giving up that which you prize the most," he cried, then his arms fell and his head bowed, and the visionary power seemed to leave him.

Cameron turned away, unable to look at him. He rubbed his face. "That's it, then. I do lose the wolf. I go back to being ordinary."

"Cameron Duffy; born of clan Ives, bargainer with Portal deities, slayer of Mrs Ferguson and bearer of the Parallel Champion – you are strong." The old man's voice was hoarse. "And together with the Wolf-

176

Boy, and the Young-Old Girl, ordinary is something you will never be."

Below, the birds were settling, leaving the sky and returning to their numerous roosts and resting places.

"I still have to beat them," said Cameron. "I have to stop Black and Grey and save the Parallel. Can't you tell me what to do?"

"I've already said more than I should." Cutler reached for a violin that lay propped against the cave wall and tucked it under his scrawny chin. "Grey will have a fight on his hands if he comes here. My birds will see to that." He drew the bow across the strings and began to play a lament so high and keening that the glass of brackish liquid vibrated in Cameron's hands.

He set it down. "Are you just going to fiddle while the Parallel fades?"

"You'd be amazed what the right notes can achieve, laddie," said Cutler as the sound died away. "Think on that. Music may be the route to my salvation, as well as your own..."

His bare foot started to tap on the earth floor as he took up his bow again. The tempo of his fiddle increased, growing faster and faster, and breaking out into a reel. As he played, the Augur danced, jigging round the cave with surprising speed. He whirled past Cameron in a blur of robes, or was it the fluttering of wings, and –

Cameron blinked.

He was on the hillside. The National Monument stood three-sided and incomplete, the troupe of bird-men gone.

He'd been returned to the Human World. Resting with their backs against a pillar were two familiar figures.

Morgan gave him a brisk nod. "Did you pass?"

"Yup."

"Good man."

Morgan's response was surprisingly subdued. Eve too looked pale and shaken.

"I have to tell you though," Cameron said. "I asked the wrong question."

"Oh *come on*." Morgan rolled his eyes. "We had a plan. Am I the only one that remembered the plan?"

"Don't be hard on him, Morgan. It's not as easy as you think. I asked a different question too. I couldn't help it." Eve gave Cameron a curious look, the meaning of which he couldn't discern. "His answer was about you and me both, Cam. And it changes everything."

CHAPTER 15

ALL SHE CARRIED
WITH HER

"So what's your greatest fear?" said Cameron, trying to break Eve's intense gaze. "Mine was pretty random."

"There was only one thing it could be." Eve sat down on the stone plinth below the pillars, drew her knees up to her chin and wrapped her arms around them protectively. "I woke up in that same tiny camp bed in the kitchen I'd slept in for years, my arms and legs sticking out everywhere. Almost immediately, the curtain across the alcove twitched and moved, reforming into that evil eight-legged face I hoped I'd never see again.

"'Such a lazy slugabed,' she growled at me. 'Idle, idle. Get up, girl. There's work to be done.'

"'Yes, Mrs Ferguson,' I said. It was like I'd never left.

"The day started like so many others.

"I scrubbed the steps. I took delivery of the raw meat that she liked to feast on. I cleaned the kitchen. I dusted and polished all her nasty little ornaments and knick knacks. And everywhere I went, she watched. From the curtains in the living room and kitchen, to the tapestry in the hall, she was always present.

"'Quite good,' she said. 'And now you will see to me. I need to be ready for my visitors.'

"'Oh no, Mrs Ferguson,' I begged. 'Must I?'

"'But of course. I must look my best. Go to the bedroom.'

"She was lying there in state, her arms folded across her chest. The old woman that I had to call my 'auntie', but was really just an empty vessel: Mrs Ferguson's human body, cold and stiff, waiting for the spider daemon to animate it.

"She was like a miser with that avatar, hoarding her minutes and hours. She knew that every time she inhabited it, it would age a little further and come closer to death.

"It always seemed to me like it was dead already.

"'Must I, must I?' I said, as I brushed its hair and looked out its clothes.

"'Pretend it's a doll, dear,' Mrs Ferguson's daemon aspect hissed from the curtains. 'Little girls like playing with dolls. Well, good little girls do, don't they? And you are good, aren't you?'

"'Yes, Mrs Ferguson.'

"'That's what I hoped. Now dress me in my finest.

Style my hair. Primp me and preen me! Make me beautiful for those who come to call.' Her spidery legs jittered with excitement..."

"I can't believe he made you go back there..." Cameron shivered. He'd first met Eve at Mrs Ferguson's flat and the horror of that place lived with him still. "Did you get any clue it wasn't real, that it was still the Augur's trial? I had these memories breaking through in mine, hints of the real world..."

"Not at first. But when I saw her avatar lying there, I started to remember. You see, it hadn't always been that old. It aged and changed while I lived with Mrs Ferguson. And eventually, it got too old altogether...

"'Mrs Ferguson,' I said, confused. 'This isn't your avatar. You wore this one out.' I struggled with the effort of recollection. 'I remember... You bid me wrap it up, and put it down in the cellar with the others.'

"The face in the curtains froze – exactly like those huge house-spiders do when they catch you looking at them out the corner of your eye.

"'Well spotted, dear. I have a replacement, don't I?' she crooned. 'Much fresher and younger than this one. Would you like to see it?'

"I nodded, thinking it couldn't be much worse than what I already had to deal with.

"'Very well, dear. Go to the kitchen. And take a look in the larder.'

"It was cold in there, in among the jams and cakes she had me bake for her respectable visitors, with the dripping joints of meat hanging from the roof.

Propped against the wall, like a spare floor-mop, was a young woman in her late teens or early twenties.

"Not exactly pretty, I thought, but striking, with an intelligent face and long dark hair.

"In the corner of the larder, a commemorative royal tea-towel had been tacked across the ventilator that gave onto the yard, preventing prying eyes from looking in. The cloth bulged and morphed, the Queen's eyes turning red as Mrs Ferguson took it over and made it spider.

"'All that she carried with her,' she said as she materialised – apropos of nothing as far as I could tell.

"I knew better than to idly question her.

"I stared at the young woman. She seemed familiar, and I liked her – not in so much as I wanted to be her friend, but in some strange way I wished to *be* her, when I grew up.

"'She's lovely,' I said. 'So much nicer than your old face.'

"'Would you like to know how I came by her? It's an amusing story. Do you recall that awful Ms Ives and her tedious grandson?'

"'Yes, Mrs Ferguson.'

"'Seven years ago, Isobel Ives came to me with a problem. Her daughter-in-law was returning from Canada. Now, this was the last thing old Ives wanted. I knew all about her squalid plans to eek out her wretched life, and who they were focussed on. If Elaine returned, there was a good chance she would persuade Ms Ives' son, Malcolm, to come away with

182

her this time, taking both him and Cameron far from Ives' reach.

"'Ives couldn't permit this to happen, and so she came to me, bearing gifts and promises. I could do whatever I wanted to divert Elaine, anything at all. She must simply never arrive.

"'I agreed. And in exchange I asked for "all that the woman carried with her."

"'Ives knew it was a suspiciously small price to pay for a banishment, so I made her bring me some pointless token as well. But she never knew the truth.'

"'The spider daemon cackled. 'All that she carried with her! As if I cared for suitcases and airport novels. But the obstinate three year old, wriggling under her arm... Elaine Duffy was bringing home her infant daughter, and that daughter would be mine. Wasn't I clever?'"

"Hold on," Cameron leapt up, interrupting Eve's narrative. "Is this for real? This isn't a messed-up alternate world thing? You're telling me I've got a sister? A baby sister I never knew about?"

Again Eve gave him that strange far-away look. "I don't know how much of the ordeal was true – but I do know the truth of this."

"Don't tell me she's still hidden away somewhere. I've got to go look for her – "

Eve smiled. "No, she's safe. I'm certain of it. Let me tell you the rest of my story, then you'll understand...

"I listened to Mrs Ferguson gloating, going on and on about how clever she was to capture this poor child. And this time I didn't agree with her. I didn't

183

meekly say, 'Yes, Mrs Ferguson.' Instead I told her what she'd done was wrong and evil. It took all my courage to stand up to her, but the daemon just shrugged it off.

"'Do you think so, dear? How delightful.' Her fiery eyes swept over the black-haired girl in the larder. 'Here she is. The child – all grown up.'

"'Seven years ago...' I frowned. 'How can that be? She's nearly twenty.'

"'Every day ages her,' said Mrs Ferguson, *'when I step inside her head.'*

"And that's when I realised: the girl was me. I was staring at myself!

"The black-haired girl vanished – or perhaps I swapped places with her, I'm not certain. All I know is my memories of the real world were coming back with a rush. The dream-ordeal was starting to break down and fall apart. I knew I was no longer the same scared little girl Mrs Ferguson had been able to bully and push about.

"'You wicked old spider,' I yelled. 'How can you still be haunting me? Morgan and Cameron dealt with you. They burnt you – they tore you down and burnt your curtain and that was the end of you.'

"'You think it's so easy to vanquish a Weaver Daemon?' she shrieked delightedly. 'You foolish child. We knit and weave our material bodies on the human plane, while our inviolable hearts remain deep in the Daemonic realm. Those boys destroyed only my earthly body. *And I have made another...'*

"She came lurching towards me, her legs skittering furiously as she tore herself free from the cloth...

"But she'd got it wrong.

"The body she'd woven from the tea-towel was small by her usual standards, and I wasn't a little girl any more.

"I was grown up.

"*Proper me.*

"Eve. As I am now.

"I grabbed the tea-towel by its corners, ripped it down, and rushed into the kitchen. It squirmed and scrabbled beneath my hands, but I ignored it. I flung the oven doors open, threw out the pastries that were cooking for Mrs Ferguson's respectable visitors

"'Stop!' the spider-daemon screamed. 'If you burn me, you'll never know the truth. I'll take it back with me to Daemonic, hide it in my hiding place. You'll never know who you really are –'

"'To be rid of you, it'll be worth it.'

"I slammed the oven door shut.

"And I woke up in the Augur's cave. I asked him who I really was. I couldn't help it, even though I think by then I already knew the answer."

Eve jumped up and put her hands on Cameron's shoulders. "Oh, don't you see, you idiot boy? There's a reason I look like you, and your horrid grandma. There's a reason that vampire judge believed our blood was connected. There's even a reason we both hear music when we world-shift. It's because you're my brother. My little big brother."

She pulled him close to her, and for a moment neither of them spoke.

Then Cameron murmured, "If I'm going to suddenly acquire a baby sister, I'm glad it's you."

"Even though I'm grumpy and bad tempered?"

"Especially because you're grumpy and bad tempered. I wouldn't have it any other way."

They stepped back, and studied each other like they'd newly met, then both broke into simultaneous smiles.

"Do you think you sort of knew, all that time ago, back at Mrs Ferguson's?" said Eve. "And that's why you helped me escape?"

Cameron snorted. "I thought you were a snotty little pain."

"Oh, what a relief. I didn't like you either."

"I don't feel like that now, obviously."

"Obviously!"

Morgan made a not-too-subtle disgusted noise, and scuffed his boot on the ground. "It's getting frosty round here. Or is it pure *slush*?"

"Morgan," Cameron gave him a hard look. "You don't exactly seem surprised?"

"That's cos I'm not. It doesn't take a genius, just a good nose. You both smell similar."

"Oh, that's gross," said Eve. "Who'd houseshare with werewolves?"

"Why didn't you say anything?" said Cameron.

Morgan shrugged. "Family's tricky. And you two already look out for each other. Would knowing have helped?" He coughed and glowered. "Anyway, is no one going to ask about my ordeal?"

"Oh poor Morgan, lovely Morgan... Don't sulk!" said Eve in an exaggerated fashion. "Tell us what happened. Where did the Augur send you? Back in time as well?"

"Nowhere."

"How do you mean?"

"Just that. It was nowhere. Like I was in a huge white featureless room, but I could never reach the edge or touch the ceiling, and the floor felt like air beneath my feet. I couldn't even tell if I was wolf or human. No sound. No smell. I tried to call out, to howl for someone, but my voice didn't work." Morgan scratched his neck. "You always need someone, when you're a wolf. Probably comes from growing up in a pack. I could tell there was no one near me there. I was totally alone."

Cameron exchanged glances with Eve. It was a long speech, by Morgan's standards, and he could tell the wolf-boy had suffered.

"You must've been scared," said Eve.

"Wasn't my finest moment."

"What did you do?" said Cameron.

"Nothing, for a really long time. I wore myself out, trying to out-run the white, searching for something to fight, to bite and claw against. In the end, I just sort of curled up and shut myself off. That's when I started to remember... I remembered you." Morgan's head hung down, a curtain of tangled fair hair shielding

187

his eyes. "Both of you, I mean. I knew you'd come for me, somehow. I knew you wouldn't leave me there. Even if I had to wait years and years, you'd find me. And that meant I wasn't really alone."

"Oh Morgan," said Eve. "What a thing to go through."

"Don't be wet." Morgan swept his hair back and glared defiantly. "Least I asked my question. Not like you dolts."

"Yes, consider that point made," said Cameron.

"Over-made, I'd say," said Eve. "Positively repetitious."

"Nah, I don't mean it really. Maybe the ordeal was easier for me, cos I already know who I am – what I am – and what I want." Morgan summoned a grin. "Right then I'd been pushed, shoved, squawked at, and shut up in an Infinite Room of Nothing, and I really, really wanted to get back at someone. I said to that scrawny wee Augur he'd better tell me how to stop the Greys, and tell me quickly or I'd see he ended up as millet for his stupid birds. Do you know what he said?"

Cameron and Eve shook their heads.

"'There's no such thing as the Greys.'

"I said, 'That's odd mate, cause I've been chased by them, and you'd better not be saying I'm lying.'

"He just waved a finger at me, and laughed. 'The wolf month is come, right enough. Uncertain is the temper of the wolf!' Then he did his mystic mojo with the birds."

"What did he tell you?"

"He said, 'There's no such thing as the Greys because the Greys are all one,' – just one overgrown fungus daemon. That makes Grey strong, because he can mobilise, command and get intel from all his offshoot blob men, but it's his big weakness too. If we can destroy the root, get rid of Grey himself, all the rest will shrivel and wither up."

"He keeps saying he wants to expand," said Cameron thoughtfully. "We've gotta make him shrink somehow. Cut him back..."

"That's not all," said Morgan. "It's the pack that's the key to it somehow. We're gonna need their help. That's what Cutler the Augur told me, before scooting me back out onto the hill. You and me, mate, we've gotta go see them. We're gonna have to take trip together – right into the heart of Dacmonic."

CHAPTER 16

INTO THE WOODS

"I've never been to Daemonic, only the Parallel. I don't even know if I could world-shift that far." Cameron frowned. "That's a big ask."

"Don't worry about it. I reckon I can get us a lift, make the transition easier." Morgan looked Cameron up and down, like he was assessing him. "You be more concerned about the pack. I wouldn't take you within sniffing distance of them if I had a choice."

"Oh come on. I've met Weres before. I survived."

"Not like these you've not. The ones that hang out on the Parallel – Lola, Eddy, Half-Tail... Grant, even – they're just kids. When Weres get old, they change. They get big and mean... Stop coming up to the Human World so much. It's like it just doesn't interest them any more. They start thinking more animal, less person. More pack." Morgan rubbed the back of his neck. "They'll see you, decide if or how you fit in, and then they'll stick to it. They don't change their minds without a fight."

"Well, they sound *charming*," said Eve, attempting to lighten the mood. "You're certain I can't come along, maybe offer some instruction on manners?"

"Not if you have any ambition of getting back intact." Morgan's green eyes regarded her humourlessly. "You may be his sister, but that doesn't make you wolf."

"No, I see that." Eve nodded briskly. "I've got things to find out anyway. I missed my chance to ask the Augur about Dr Black, and I want to make up for that. I can do research, and see what I find about him – and anything about the World Engine too."

"Good plan." Cameron patted his jacket, and drew out the compact shape of Montmorency's netbook. "All of my browser tabs should still be open. That'll give you a headstart."

"Thanks." Eve took the computer. She gave Cameron a shrewd look. "You haven't told us, you know. About your ordeal."

"I asked what's gonna happen to me. With my wolf-side, you know? I'm not sure I fully understood the answer. But it looks like I don't have it forever. I can only win by giving it up."

Morgan's mouth opened, like he wanted to say something then thought the better of it. His brow furrowed. "Doesn't work like that, mate. You don't get a choice. You just are. Trust me on this. There isn't a cure."

191

Cameron looked away. He shrugged, trying to appear as if he didn't care about the loss of the wolf, when really it was almost all he could think about. "Hey, I'm not the Mystic All-Seeing Augur. It's not my stupid prediction."

"But that's good, isn't it?" Eve interjected in a soothing tone. "That means you'd be human again."

"Thanks," Morgan rumbled. "So much."

Eve shot him an exasperated glance. "I didn't mean it like that! I just meant Cameron doesn't have to go running about mad and furry once a month for the rest of his life."

"Why not? If that's what I want?"

"You get to be normal."

"What makes you think," Cameron said quietly, "I'd ever want that?"

They glared at each other for a moment, then Eve threw up her hands. "Maybe you don't. But *you* didn't grow up living with a daemon. You had thirteen years before it all turned freaky. Thirteen years with your dad – my dad too, it turns out – to look out for you. Remember that."

"Eve... normal's not all that great. I miss Dad, sure, but you still get problems in the human world, and hard times, and bad people, and things going wrong, and –"

"Grey blobs trying to absorb you?" Eve shook her head. "Maybe it isn't that brilliant, but maybe I'd like my own chance to find out." She turned and started to walk down the hill. "I'll meet you two back at the house."

192

Cameron ran after her. "What about the wards? It's not secure back there."

"I'll make the biggest pot of coffee you've ever seen. Nothing is creeping up on me while I doze. And besides," Eve ran a hand through her hair, "I'm not afraid of spider-daemons any more."

"Glad to hear it."

She stopped and gave him an apologetic smile. "Be careful, won't you?"

"*Me*, be careful? I thought you were my little sister?"

"Your big little sister." She drew herself up to her full height. "And don't you forget it." She walked away without a glance back.

"When did Miss Sensible get so grown up?" Morgan said over Cameron's shoulder. They watched Eve continue on the path towards town, a newly confident spring in her step.

"I dunno. It just sort of happened." Cameron squinted and gave a rueful grin. "Now, about this lift?"

Morgan gestured towards the streaming blur of lights that indicated the distant traffic of Princes Street. "We go that way... We're gonna let the train take the strain."

Beneath the girders of Waverley Station's expansive glass roof, a hustle of evening commuters made their way home. No one seemed to notice the two boys fighting the flow of the crowds. They neither boarded a train, bought a ticket, nor stopped to look for friends – but instead appeared fascinated by the station's grand Victorian architecture.

"This is all a bit Potter, isn't it?" said Cameron as they headed down the concourse. He noticed Morgan's blank expression. "Platform 9¾? Magic train to Hogwarts?"

"Huh?"

"Seriously? How can you not know Harry Potter?"

Morgan curled his lip in a mock snarl and jabbed a thumb at his incisors. "Werewolf. Remember?"

"You used to live in a cinema."

"Which fell out of the Human World and into the Parallel fifty years ago. We weren't exactly on trend. Now would you shut up and help me find this tunnel?" Morgan lifted his nose. "This place stinks of coffee cups and electricity."

"Not steam and devious Roman deities?" said Cameron. "Remind me precisely why you think Janus is going to help?"

"Said he'd be seeing me again, didn't he? Before he dropped me splat in the snow."

"And Janus doesn't say anything without a reason..."

"Exactly." Morgan stopped and glared. "The Parallel Line climbs up from Scotland Street, and it's meant to terminate here... But this is all too new." He tapped a diminutive station attendant on the shoulder, drawing her attention. "All your trains go in and out – not up and down. What's wrong with them?"

"That's novel. People usually complain about times, not direction." The woman gave him a kindly smile, as if humouring a lost child. "Are you all right, love?"

"Morgan, leave the lady alone." Cameron grabbed his arm and dragged the glowering teenager away. "Over here!"

At the far end of the opposite side of the platform, fenced off from passengers and standing at right angles to the existing train track, was a small iron gate. A metal sign set into the wall indicated it marked the site of 'the original Edinburgh – Leith – Newhaven Railway'.

"Huh... how d'you spot that?"

Cameron tapped the corner of his eye. "Can't always be about the nose. Let's world-shift and check it out."

He focussed on the Parallel Tune and watched the world reassemble...

The commuters faded, leaving the station empty of people. The glass roof above now revealed the ragged, tangled landscape of the Parallel, the buildings' windows dark and empty. Here too, the Greys' intimidation tactics seemed to have taken hold.

The iron gate vanished, the opening behind stretching into a tunnel mouth, which disgorged a rolling nimbus of smoke tinged with reddish light. The distant thunder of pistons betrayed the approach of The January Express.

"How's that gonna work? It's not coming in sideways, is –" Cameron lurched as the ground beneath his feet shifted. The platform – and the rails alongside it – were rotating through 90 degrees. It was like they were standing on the arm of a giant clock that had decided to swing abruptly from quarter to half past the hour.

Morgan hooked one arm around a pillar and deftly grabbed Cameron's collar with the other, catching him before he stumbled toward the tracks. "Hold up! Wait for the train, eh?"

"Oh, you know..." Cameron shot him a grateful glance. "Thought I'd get in early doors."

The rails were now aligned with the Parallel tunnel. They locked into place just as The January Express hove into sight.

A head wearing a driver's cap popped out of the cab. Janus lifted a set of goggles with four darkened lenses, and propped them onto his smoke-blackened forehead. "Hello, wolf-boys... Fancy a ride?"

"We're heading to the wolven forest of the Black Hills – in Daemonic," Morgan shouted over the scream of brakes. "You'd need to turn this lump of metal round, go back through the Parallel Interchange... That ok for you?"

"I am always happy to go both directions," said Janus's left face.

His right face raised an eyebrow. "The replacement governor valve needs a run-in anyway. It is a challenge to source proper Makaris-built parts..."

"Such a *bore* the Makaris all died out," interjected left. "Spares are so hard to find."

196

A ruthless grin spread across right's face. "Although we did have the foresight to set a spare valve by, some years before their unfortunate demise."

"Is it too late to walk?" Cameron hissed out the side of his mouth to Morgan. "He's unhinged."

Morgan biffed him lightly on the arm. "It'll be fine." He raised his voice. "Lift would be appreciated, mighty Janus."

Janus swung himself down from the cab, nodding to a marble statue of a toga-wearing man to take his place. The statue, which seemed to Cameron to have a rather feline set to its features, inclined its head, moved over and stepped behind the controls.

Janus marched along the length of the red and gold train, eyeing the steaming, clicking mechanism with approval. "The garden room is closed for repairs, but we'll make do in here." He threw open a door on the first carriage, revealing the impossibly large space of the Temple of the Door. "After you!"

They stepped aboard. Cameron felt the vibration of the engine increase and the sensation of motion as the rails began to rotate, swinging round to re-orientate the front of the train with the tunnel from which it had emerged.

"Next stop: Daemonic." Janus drew a salver of water and began to scrub the oil and grease from his twin faces.

The engine took on a laboured note as it descended the steep incline of the tunnel. The yellow illumination of Waverley station receded, replaced

197

by a reddish radiance that steadily increased, bathing the carriage in hellish light.

The Song of the Parallel sprang unbidden into Cameron's mind. He clutched his head in pain, his fingers pushing hard into the bones behind his ears.

If the tune he usually heard was a stripped down live performance, then this felt like a full-volume rocked-out album version with feedback and distortion.

"It's – happening. We're – shifting – through."

"Relax, mate," said Morgan. "It won't last."

"Easy for you to say." In the background of the song, the wolf howl that had come to haunt Cameron seemed to have been replaced with an excited chorus of yips and whines. He groaned. "It's absolutely barking stars in my head right now!"

The intensity of the music built. It reached a single immense crashing chord, then all at once – like the moment when pressure finally equalises in a climbing aircraft – it was over.

Cameron stretched his jaw and sighed with relief.

"Cheer up," said Morgan. "That was the easy part."

Janus shook water from his hands, the droplets falling blood-like to the salver in the red interior glow. "And how have you been faring with the Omniclavis?" He looked up into the murky air at the drifting portal outlines. For a moment, the compact shape of an office door with frosted-glass flickered into existence, followed by the image of a feather caught floating between two tall stone columns. "Hogg's chambers, I see, and then the

Augury... One more to go! You'll get to the *heart* of the problem yet."

"Was that another hint?" Cameron muttered darkly.

"More a suggestion. It would suit me to see Grey and Black's plans fall apart," said left face.

"Watt's too. I would have him brought to a halt," right added pointedly.

"Oh, I'm getting sick of all this," said Cameron. Morgan shot him a warning glance but he continued unabashed. "You and the Augur both! I bet you know all about what me and Morgan and Eve have had to face – the Court, the lump, the ordeals..."

"Of course."

"Then why "

"Why did I make you go through it? Why? Why?" Janus's left face lifted his voice into a nasal whine, parodying Cameron's. For a moment, the train seemed to stutter and skip a beat on the tracks.

"Because I'm a God of Journeys, aren't I, you little fool?" roared right. "And this is your journey."

"You should be grateful," left smirked. "You get to travel this part in style."

"Oh yeah?" Cameron blasted back. "Well think about this – if Grey and Black run their World Engine, there isn't going to *be* a Parallel any more – let alone a route between Daemonic and the Human World. One trashed carriage will be the least of your problems. You're not going to get to run around playing trains much longer."

Janus stalked towards the window, spread his arms

and pressed his fingers against the glass. Outside, the gloom of the Parallel tunnel had given way to the Daemon World. Unknown things wheeled and swooped in a burnt umber sky, below which rolled a dark landscape of wooded hills and valleys, covered in thick snow.

"For as long as humans and daemons can stack stone and wood and build shelter, I will exist: the Guardian of all Portals. Do not doubt it! My power pre-dates the Parallel, and will outlast it too..." He paused for a moment then added in quieter tones, "But I don't take kindly to those who would derail me."

"Then tell us," Cameron urged. "Tell us what I need to do to beat them."

"It is tempting... But you must know every prophecy has a price." Janus's fingers rapped contemplatively on the glass. "Very well! This is what I'll do. I'll tell one of you." He turned back to face Cameron and Morgan, all four eyes sparkling with malicious amusement.

"One of us?" Cameron frowned. "But what's to stop him immediately telling the other?"

"Nothing." A grin unfurled across Janus's two faces. "Nothing at all. If that's what he wants."

"Then –"

"No deal." Morgan stepped forward, moving closer to Cameron. "We don't work like that."

"But Morgan... What if this is the chance we need? To stop Black and Grey *and* save my wolf-side?"

"There's a catch – don't you see?" Morgan's eyes

blazed bright and green. "Secrets won't work out for us. It's gotta be both – or nothing."

"No. I remember..." Cameron nodded and turned back to Janus. "No deal, Janus. We'll have to solve this for ourselves."

"What an excellent partnership! It'd be sad to see it split apart." Janus clapped a hand to either face. "Oh dear! Sometimes my mouth just *runs* away with me."

"I'm not going anywhere," said Morgan stubbornly. "So don't pretend I am."

"No?"

"Me neither," said Cameron. "We're a team."

"How touching! Well, that accounts for two of you," said Janus. "What about the third?"

"Eve will stick by us too," said Morgan. "She's a good kid. She's sound."

"I'm not speaking of her." Janus threw back his head and laughed. "Times they are a changing, boys. Even a wolf month can't last forever. You have very few howls left, and then it's over." He snapped his fingers. "Understand?"

The train dropped them by a frozen pond at the base of a hill. Janus conjured a doorway and hustled them out into the snow.

"Off you go, into the woods," he said with wry amusement. "Come see me again. I may have a 'reward' for you, if you punish those who tried to hijack my Express... A new ward, even. Wouldn't that be apt?"

"I saw the price you asked for that last time." Cameron shivered as he stepped into the cold air. "It wasn't one I'm willing to pay."

"Prices change. By then a sacrifice will have been made."

As the train pulled away, Cameron stared at the tracks running in straight black lines into the distance.

"I've had it up to here with predictions." He liked to think he was making his own choices, but it felt like he kept being dragged back, forced onto someone else's path... "Everyone's saying I have to lose the wolf, that the Parallel's gonna take it back somehow. What if I don't want that? What if I still want to be me?"

Morgan took off his prized army greatcoat, bundled it up, and stashed it behind a tree. "You'll be you."

"You mean I can change things? I don't have to go back to being normal?"

"Didn't say that. I just meant..." He paused in the process of removing his sweater and t-shirt, checking the Omniclavis was cinched tight on the cord around his neck. "Why do you think you'd be normal without the wolf? I knew you before, and you were all kinds of weird."

"Remind me why we're friends again?"

"Never figured that one out." Morgan grinned lopsidedly.

"It's a big thing to give up though," Cameron persisted. "What if I don't choose to let it go?"

"Then bye-bye Parallel?" Morgan shrugged.

"You reckon the Augur's right, then? That's the choice?" Cameron picked at the laces of his trainers with numb fingers. "I suppose there *is* always a choice..."

"Not always. Some stuff you only get to run away from for so long... And on that happy note – now you get to meet the family. Aren't you lucky?"

"I dunno. Am I?"

"Nah, not really. *Beware of the dogs.* You'd better let me do the talking." Morgan stretched and looked warily around at the forested hills. "Long time since I shifted outside of a Fat Moon... Gotta be some advantage to coming home, I guess."

He leapt up, his arms pointed to the sky, white fur springing thickly from his skin. By the time his hands and feet hit the ground again, all four were paws.

Almost invisible against the snow, a sleek white wolf began to pad up the hill, scenting out a hidden path. Moments later, moving behind it like a shadow, came its counterpart: the black wolf that was Cameron Duffy.

CHAPTER 17

WOLF HALL

Black paws on white snow...

The ground beneath your pads is hard and crisp.

Easy to slip on, so claws spread wide, but it's firmer than the deeper drifts – more of a kickback from your hind legs – so you can go swift.

Ears twitch, eyes scan: left to right, down to the ground, then back to the horizon. White wolf in front of you, almost in camouflage with the snow, but you scent-see him – know him – instantly.

Morgan.

He turns to look at you, his eyes urging caution, so you bring your head down, press your body low to the ground, make your profile as slight as possible...

It's hard to keep yourself so contained.

Over the past year, on those three glorious moon-blessed nights a month, you've adventured through woods in the Parallel, and in the quieter parts of the Human World too, but this place offers something new...

You draw in scent, and information leaps in your mind: every tiny trace a key-note of the whole it comes from. There's something furtive and squirrelly concealed near by, and your paws *itch* with the effort of trying not to instantly hunt it. Next, you sense something warm and burrowing that your stomach believes would make good eating. Eager saliva wells in your cheeks, and you swallow impulsively. Meanwhile, out in the darkness, there are creatures deadlier than you, waiting with infinite patience to have your heart...

Daemon prey – and Daemon predator. It's all here...

But there's something still more exciting too.

Woven into the path, in a track that stretches back thousands of Fat Moons, you detect others of your kind. Werewolf after werewolf has climbed this way – with empty bellies and bellies stretched taut, in joy and in terror – but always as part of a greater whole. This intrigues you in ways you don't fully understand. It speaks to you of safety, of comradeship and warmth; it offers the possibility of collective strength and power.

It is intoxicating.

It is *overwhelming*.

The howl leaves your jaws before you can stop yourself.

It echoes round the bowl of trees and out across the dark red Daemonic sky – a resonant musical cry. Its meaning: *I am here! I am here! Where are you? Where are you?*

Morgan turns to you in alarm: ears back, eyes wide, teeth parted. *What have you done?* He's scanning the surroundings for cover, somewhere to lay low, but already the howl is answered.

The forest speaks with its wolf-voice: low and high and multiple and all-together, the howl returns... Its meaning: *We are here! We are here! And we are many.*

The night fills with eyes.

You don't try to fight or run.

The newcomers are huge, muscled hunters. They are controlling: herding you and Morgan with low growls, circling round and driving you up the hill. They are deferential as well, surprisingly. Morgan has only to curl a lip and they drop back. But still – by force of numbers – they push you on.

On the hilltop, a low hall lies, its blackened wood scented with long-dried sap. You are guided to an entrance by your escorts. You and Morgan pass within, and your wolf-self retreats.

You are human once more.

It was the easiest wolf-shift Cameron could ever remember, like shrugging off a warm and comfortable coat. He stretched, feeling shivery and ill-at-ease in his human skin despite the fire-lit ambience of the hall.

He was standing in an antechamber that seemed to

serve as a cloakroom. Coats and jackets and shoes and boots were littered round its edges.

Their escort had remained outside, patrolling. The white wolf beside him reared on its hind legs and became Morgan again.

"Had to go and howl, didn't you?" Morgan scowled. "Just couldn't help yourself, could you?"

"No, I couldn't. It felt true. Like I was meant to call them to me. Like I belonged."

"They'll make you belong all right... You could be happily safe and *bored* here for the rest of your natural, as long as you do exactly what's expected."

Cameron shrugged. "We were coming here anyway, weren't we?"

"Yeah. But I wanted to do it on my own terms."

A bearded red-haired man approached. He was tall – easily over two-and-a-half metres, Cameron reckoned – but he held himself in an awkward pose, with his head lowered and arms pressed to his sides.

He handed Morgan a rich embroidered cloak, which the boy took and put on with barely a glance. The man repeated the gesture to Cameron, then returned with water in leather flagons and some cuts of meat. Morgan lifted a leg bone and made short work of it – hungry as ever after the shift. He tossed the gnawed end to the floor and the man, after waiting a moment to be sure it wasn't wanted, lifted the discarded bone and stowed it in the folds of his jerkin.

"What's up with him?" Cameron hissed. "More to the point, what's up with you?"

"He's an Omega. Subservient. Thinks his place is to defer."

"To you? Is that why you're acting like a complete –"

"Power structures and bloodlines are important in the pack. Because my mum is Alpha Female, I get deference. Pathetic, isn't it?"

The red-headed man obsequiously presented Cameron with the plate of meat. Cameron helped himself to a bone. "Why do I get the rock-star treatment, then?"

"Tell him. Go on." Morgan instructed the bearded man.

The man looked at Cameron uneasily. His jittery agitation reminded Cameron of a red-setter dog whose tail was lashing from side to side: as if you'd stepped into his house, but he hadn't quite decided if you were welcome or not.

"You're with him, aren't you? Aren't you? Under his protection? That makes you important too... Aren't you important?"

"Very," Morgan growled. "Don't you forget it."

The man cringed and backed off. "No, no. I wouldn't do that."

Morgan raised an eyebrow and studied Cameron. "Still think you want a pack? That you belong?"

"I dunno. Part of me does..." Cameron scratched his neck through the woven cloth of his robe. In his human body, his wolfish thoughts and urges were on the retreat again. "It's complicated."

Morgan looked sceptical. "They're not all as easily

impressed as friend Omega. Let's get this over with. Remember – I'll do the talking."

They moved into the main section of the hall. Round the edges of the room, a dozen children play-fought with sticks and bones, while old people dozed by the fire. Low tables and benches were covered with the scattered remains of a banquet, around which men and women in hempen robes ate and talked and laughed. They were physically larger than average, at least for humans, with long tangled hair and a powerful, slightly hunched-over posture that reminded Cameron of hackles: the ruffs of fur that rose up on wolves' backs.

The Were-people looked at him and Morgan with shielded eyes, noting their presence while keeping their attention pointedly focussed elsewhere. They seemed a different lot to the Weres he'd encountered elsewhere on the Parallel, camped in the old Alhambra Cinema where Morgan used to hang out. It suddenly hit Cameron that everyone here was an adult or a young child.

There was no one in-between.

He snuck a glance at Morgan. He'd said that Weres changed as they grew older – would that count for him as well? Would Morgan lose his passion for rock music, for adventure... for the Human World altogether? Would he become another wannabe Viking, like this strange group?

"Here he comes, our noble stepson; the lone wolf and relic thief..." A mocking voice rang out, and the general hubbub in the room faded, as if someone had dipped a volume control.

At the end of the hall, on a raised dais were two wooden thrones carved with moon and holly symbols. A man with a clippered goatee and a dark saturnine look sat on one, while a flaxen-haired woman occupied the other, a simple silver circlet resting on her head. Her fierce green eyes and pointed cheekbones made clear her family connection to Morgan.

"I'm not going to let him rile me, I'm not," Morgan muttered to himself, his fists clenched by his side. He approached the dais. Cameron followed, acutely aware that since the Wolf King had acknowledged their presence, everyone in the room was openly staring.

The Wolf Queen caught his eye for a second. She shifted on her throne, and he just noticed the spine of a worn paperback book – *The Picture of Dorian Gray* – before she covered it over with a fur. It was the only glimpse of modern life he'd seen inside the hall.

"Two visits in less than a week. We are indeed honoured," the Wolf King continued. He eyed Morgan dispassionately. "We could almost mistake this for enthusiasm – were it not for the fact you had to be brought here under escort. Do you think that is appropriate behaviour?"

"Wouldn't come at all if I could help it," said Morgan cheerfully. "Not to see you anyway."

"*You forget your place!*"

"Ok, ok. I defer. You're the King," Morgan drawled. He bobbed an insincere bow. "But this isn't about you and me, and who gets the most bones. It's about the Parallel... It's shutting down and fading out –"

"We know. We have seen."

"If Dr Black and Mr Grey get to run their World Engine, it'll be gone for good. We need the pack's help to stop them."

"How does this concern us?" The Wolf King lifted a jewelled hand and gestured expansively. "Our domain is here in Daemonic. The humans have their metal-snarled world – and welcome to it. As for the Parallel..." His hand fell to the side of his throne. "A half-place. A mistake. A mixed-up zone, filled and fuelled by sad wanderers who belong to neither true world. Let these Grey and Black creatures do with it what they will."

"You can't mean that!" Cameron burst out. "You've got to help. The Parallel affects us all!"

"What do you know of our history, human-born?" The Wolf King leant forward, his upper lip stretched taut to expose his teeth. "Those who travel between the worlds, be they daemon or human, what do they have in common?"

"The Parallel Inheritance, of course," Cameron said, uncertain what the King was driving at.

"Which means what?"

"Which means we are descended from those in Mitchell and Astredo's covens, from the World Split conspiracy... They looked into the Parallel as it formed, and that connected them to it forever. That's how we can world-shift." Cameron gave a hard smile. "I know the story. I'm not a newbie."

"The shifting was a *side-effect*, not the intention," the Wolf King snarled. "Those who supported the World Split plan were separatists, who believed our interests would be better served if humans and daemons lived apart." He glowered at the assembled Weres whose heads swiftly bowed in response. "It is a bitter irony that I preside over a pack who may still travel to the Human World, when our ancestor wished instead to keep us safely isolated."

They looked like they're being told off for bunking off school, thought Cameron, glancing round the hall. He wondered how many of the pack might secretly miss their excursions through the Parallel...

"If some fungus-daemon and his pet human wish to destroy a sordid back-alley that leads out to a world of danger and distraction, I have no objection. My pack will not interfere." The Wolf King sat back in his chair, seemingly basking in his dominance. "Let the Parallel die."

"Knew we shouldn't have come," Morgan spat. "So much for the Augur! Looks like his crystal ball was out of warranty. Come on, Cam. We're better off without them." He turned on his heel and started to march down the hall.

"Wait. You do not have leave to go." The Wolf Queen's voice was soft, but the authority it wielded was clear. Several of the largest Were-people rose from their benches and moved to block off the exit.

"Seriously?" said Morgan. "You're gonna keep us here? Is that what it's come to?"

"I merely wish the pleasure of your company a little longer, my son."

Morgan looked dubious. "Then call off your guards."

The Queen rubbed her forehead and managed a patient smile. "Tell us, at least, who the friend is you have brought with you?" She indicated Cameron. "He is Were-kind, I sense it, but not one of us."

"The boy is without a pack – not born a wolf at all," the King sneered. "My spies tell me everything. Just another half-breed liability who will run wild at Fat Moon, spreading our legend in the Human World until our existence is known to all." His arms folded across his chest. "It would be best he is not allowed to return to it."

Cameron felt his stomach tighten. The guards who had stood up earlier were moving closer, striding purposefully down the hall. His mouth went dry. Even if he made it outside, the patrol would be waiting...

"If he was not born a wolf, then he must've been gifted our heritage," said the Queen. "Who would do something so dangerous?"

"Your son. Who else?" the King retorted. "He bites indiscriminately. Another sign he is not fit to succeed –"

"I believe he is." The Wolf Queen's eyes flashed a baleful green. She swept down from the dais. At her unspoken cue, the lumbering guards halted.

"I will hear his reasons." She placed a pale hand under Morgan's chin and raised it. "Tell me, Morgan, my wolfheart... Did you make this human prey to the Fat Moon?"

213

"I did." Morgan jerked his head away, avoiding her gaze. "I'd do it again too."

The Wolf Queen looked sad. "I thought I'd raised you better."

"He saved my life! I begged him to do it," Cameron interjected forcefully. "That's the only reason... Don't blame him! If he hadn't bitten me, I'd be dead. I owe him *everything* – and I don't regret it for a second."

"Is this true?"

"He's saved my life too... more than once," said Morgan. "There was a time I was moon-mad. If anyone was in danger of going wild and drawing notice, it was me." A horrified murmur ran around the room. "Cam looked after me till it passed, and I could re-learn how to master my instincts. That's not all. He stopped me being food for Mrs Ferguson, and put an end to that toxic old Weaver, and –"

"He's resourceful then," the Wolf King stroked his goatee and mused. "I could use a deputy with fire and imagination. A new Beta perhaps, or a general in waiting... But we still cannot let him go." He gestured sharply. "Have them locked up, until I decide my course of action."

A thick-set guard pushed forward, trying to grab for Cameron's arms. Without even thinking he reacted...

...and shifted.

A claw swiped at the guard. Cameron's loose cloak fell away as he dropped to all fours in wolf-form. A terrible growl reverberated round the hall, challenging anyone that dared approach him.

"Is that meant to impress? The yelpings of a cub?" The Wolf King laughed. "You may scare humans, but here in Daemonic, we shift at will." His lip curled. "If I showed my wolf face to you, then you would know terror. You would quiver like the cur you are." He snapped his fingers. "Take him away and teach him some respect. I grow weary."

"It's not like that!" Morgan shouted, wrestling with the guard who was trying to pin him down. "Cameron's different! He's not like any of us! He can shift whenever he wants – wherever he is – in the Parallel and up in the Human World! *He's the strongest werewolf I've ever seen!*"

A hush fell upon the crowd. The guards froze. All eyes turned to the Alphas.

"Lies." The King waved a dismissive hand. "Desperate half-truths, snatched from the stories pups are told in the litter."

"No." The Queen shook her head. "I don't believe so. There is honesty in my son's words. I scent it."

"What is this? You dare defy me?" The Wolf King's face reddened, his teeth bared.

"No, my dear," the Queen replied calmly. "To defy you, I would need first to be subject to your will... And that I have never been."

The King's mouth dropped open. He and the Queen stared at each other, the air tense with an unspoken battle for control. Then, abruptly, he sat down upon his throne.

The Queen turned back to Cameron and Morgan, her expression unreadable. "There is one way to seek the truth of this – I would see it for myself."

CHAPTER 18

BEHIND THE SCENES
AT THE MUSEUM

Cameron shivered in his robes, pulling them close to his human body. They were on top of Blackford Hill, back in the Human World, the night clinging cold and dark around them. Cameron had recognised his surroundings at once, spotting the familiar turret of the Observatory. His gran's house was tantalisingly near – Eve was most likely there now. He looked wistfully towards the road that led down to it. He felt like he was so nearly home, yet so far away...

The Queen sniffed the air. She and the King, practised at shifts between the worlds, had brought Morgan and Cameron back, transporting through the Parallel with ease. She walked across the grass, the frost apparently not affecting her bare feet, and spoke quietly to her son. "It's been years since I was last here. Do you remember how your father and I would bring you, when you were just a pup? And we would run and run across the hills, without a care?"

He nodded.

"I had to teach you about this world too if you were to live in it, at least for a time. I do not think it is such a bad place."

The Wolf King made a derisive sound.

"*He* doesn't agree," said Morgan.

"If we were only meant to live as wolves, then why do we have a human face at all?" She looked up at the cloud-covered sky. "On some nights, human is all I can be. All I want to be, even."

"Let us see the boy do different," the King said. "If he can."

Cameron looked desperately to Morgan. "I've never shifted like this before. It's always happened by instinct, because I was in desperate need of it. I can't just call it up. I don't know what to do!"

"Believe me, mate, you need it now," said Morgan. "If you want to save the Parallel you've gotta prove him wrong. So try your best. Show him who's boss."

Cameron closed his eyes, turning the focus of his mind inward. *I hope you know what's at stake here, Parallel Champion, because I don't reckon we're going to get a second chance...* He tried to think wolfish thoughts, remembering the rush of sensation that had accompanied his run through the Daemonic woods: the quickened pulse of blood in his veins, the forest mapped out in scent trails stretching back into the past, the excitement of being simultaneously hunter and hunted.

He opened his eyes.

His perspective had changed. He was lower, more firmly anchored to the ground, his vision sharper. Stranger still, the Wolf King was bowed on one knee before him, a look of barely contained fury on his face.

It had worked. Cameron was wolf.

And the Wolf King smelled of fear...

"So you can shift outside the Fat Moon, even in the Human World. Your power," the King said through gritted teeth, "exceeds my own. I am forced, reluctantly, to recognise you as Alpha."

"So you're giving in without a fight?" Morgan crossed his arms over his chest and crowed. "Look who's the big wolf now..."

"Not to you," the King spat. "You'll never lead. To him."

"It is the challenger's right to name the place of battle," the Queen said simply. "If Cameron elected to fight in this world as wolf, my husband would be mere human, so the boy's strength would be greater." She moved to stand beside the King. "See, my husband? Sometimes our human side has its advantages. Diplomacy saves blood-spill."

Cameron shook, his fur rippling. He raised himself onto his hind legs and felt the wolf lift from him, as lightly as if a veil of silk had been drawn from over his face. It didn't seem entirely right for the shift to be so easy, so effortless. The simplicity of it scared him.

It was as if the wolf was already disconnecting, and starting to slip away from his grasp...

He stretched and re-fastened the woven robe he'd been given in the hall.

"The pack is yours," the King said in a monotone. He was still kneeling, his eyes lowered. "Do with it as you please."

"Get up."

The King's brow furrowed, and for a moment he looked fearful. "But I've given it to you. I've handed it over –"

"I said, get up. You don't have to bow to me. What would I want a pack for anyway?" Cameron looked over at Morgan and shrugged. "I mean – what would I do with them? Imagine that lot hanging about the house all the time, mooching and growling. Eve'd be furious. She thinks two of us is bad enough."

Morgan's face was a picture of mock outrage. "Oh *come on*. At least order him to run about barking first, or make him stand on one leg for a bit... just for laughs?"

Cameron shook his head. "Nah. You were right. I don't want to belong to anything that's about ordering people about, keeping them in line. I don't hold with that in any world." He remembered the ordeal of the Augur, that Odyssey warehouse Grey had made him work in: all those long straight lines, boxes and boxes pressing down on him... then one brilliant moment of music, of rebellion, that set him free...

"The Parallel's the thing." He turned back to the

King. "You're going to help me save it. That's my condition. The Augur said you could stop Grey, and I need to hold you to that."

The King nodded his agreement, his expression still a little grudging. "We will come at your call. At your time of greatest need, the pack will be there. I swear it."

He turned and strode away, fading from the hillside as he shifted back to Daemonic. The Queen lingered, glancing from Morgan to Cameron. "Our legends say the Moon-free are rare, and their time is very short." She reached out and placed both hands on Cameron's shoulders, almost as if she was giving him some kind of blessing. "I think the Wolf will leave you soon. Embrace it while you can," she said; then she too was gone.

"Wins a pack – then just gives it away." Morgan let out a long low whistle. "That was quite something. Either utterly brilliant or totally daft, I'm not sure which. What do you reckon?"

"I reckon we should be getting back to Eve," said Cameron, starting to head down the hill. "Let's see what she's found out."

Lights were blazing in the windows of the house on Observatory Row, and in the garden smoked the remains of a bonfire. They found Eve in the kitchen, surrounded by a laptop, a fire poker and a dozen dirty coffee cups. Rather incongruously, she was wearing a sleek black evening dress, and had her hair piled up elegantly on top of her head.

"Eve," said Cameron, "you look..."

"Ridiculous?"

"Older, I was going to say. Grown-up."

"I hardly know what age I feel any more... I've been raiding your gran's – our gran's, I mean – wardrobe again. She must've been very glamorous once."

"Yeah. Back when dinosaurs roamed the earth." Cameron foraged wearily in the fridge for food.

"Been doing a bit of decorating?" Morgan pointed a thumb at the window, which, like the others in the house, had been stripped bare of coverings.

"I made a fire and burnt them all, to prevent further attacks by Weavers."

"Drastic," said Cameron approvingly, between mouthfuls of chicken drumstick.

"You know there's all kinds of other beasties out there, right?" said Morgan. "Not just Weavers?"

"Oh, yes." Eve waved the poker. "I'm prepared. I've got advance warning." She indicated the bone necklace the Selkie woman had given her at the daemon market, which was hanging off a hook by the kitchen towels. "This isn't as useless as *some people* claimed. Turns out it lets you know if something nasty is about to world-shift into your home." Her nose wrinkled. "Mainly by giving off a sudden smell of rotting fish."

Morgan looked bashful. "What do I know about selkie magic? How did you find that out?"

"How do you think? That's why I annihilated the curtains."

"Ouch. You *are* pretty fierce when you want to be, aren't you?"

"Never doubt it. There's been nothing since then. I think they're all too busy fleeing from the mayhem Grey's causing." She raised an eyebrow. "Good visit home to see the folks?"

"Better than I expected," said Morgan, checking whether Cameron had left him any chicken. "The pack're gonna come when they're called, help us sort out old fungus features. Turns out Cam's their new Alpha."

"That's me." Cameron gave a modest smile. "Top Dog."

"My brother the wolf lord. Am I expected to bow?"

"Not all the time."

"Too kind. My, it's all happening, isn't it? Let me show you what I've discovered." She swivelled the laptop round to face the boys. A picture of Dr Black's thin face was captioned: Our keynote speaker, Dr Alasdair Black, who will present a paper that he claims will rewrite our understanding of the universe.

"He's appearing at a conference called, 'Looking into Dark Matters'. I think that's supposed to be an astronomer joke." Eve pulled a face. "They've been talking shop at the University all day, then they have a big reception this evening at the Museum of Scotland. Black's speech is being saved for after dinner, like he's the star event." She clicked to another tab. "Look at what he's called it."

Morgan read the title aloud. "World Split: A Radical New Vision of the Origins of the Earth, and its Potential Parallel."

Cameron whistled. "He's not going to get much more radical than telling everyone the truth about the Human and Daemon Worlds –"

"How about running a World Engine that's gonna knock out the Parallel hidden between them?" said Morgan. "That'd wake them all up."

"Precisely." Eve exchanged a serious look with her friends. "I think that's what he's planning to do. I'm guessing the World Engine must be hidden there somewhere, so he can set if off at the climax to his big speech."

The colour drained from Cameron's face. "Imagine if he succeeds... The last route of magic from Daemonic to Humanian closes, and he's telling a room full of scientists they're now living in a world where *everything* can be explained, understood and controlled. He's starting something big and it's starting tonight."

At the back of his mind, a familiar howl of indignation sounded. *The wolf was restless once more...* It made him feel unsettled, but at the same time he knew it was a positive sign. It meant they were on the right track.

He jumped to his feet. "We've got to get down there and stop him."

Eve stood up too. "Why do you suppose," she said, a touch theatrically, "I'm dressed like this?"

"For a laugh? Because you want to look smart for

223

the world ending?" Cameron scratched the back of his head and grimaced. "How should I know?"

Eve sighed. "I went up to the Observatory earlier. That's where Black studied, so they know all about him and his work. I said I was his sister, in town to see his big night, but I'd lost my invitation, and could they possibly help?"

"And they just believed you?" said Cameron.

"I was standing on top of Blackford Hill in an evening dress in the middle of winter – of course they believed me! What was more likely – a misplaced invite, or I was one of a plucky band of rebels trying to stop Black's work?"

"Eve, you are spectacular." Cameron punched the air, then just as swiftly grabbed his sister for a hug.

"Aren't I? But I only got one invite, so I'm going to have to smuggle you two in." She pulled away, noticing the woven robes both boys had brought back from Daemonic. "What *do* you think you're wearing?"

A low barrier separated the outside stairs to the museum's basement from the thoroughfare of the street. Cameron and Morgan ducked under it and crept down to the gate below. It rattled in Morgan's hand. "Locked. Will I use the Omniclavis? We've got one shot left."

"Hmm, not sure," said Cameron. "That stuff

Janus said about getting to the heart of the mystery – I somehow don't reckon he meant a back gate."

"Does it matter as long as it gets us in? We're gonna need to hurry up."

"I know." Cameron glanced up to the street, but they were well in the shadows and no one appeared to be taking any notice. "Eve's not going to be able to sneak away forever."

"Why don't you wolf it?"

"You what?"

"If you can shift any time, why don't you call up your superior firepower right now?"

Cameron stared at him. "That's not entirely a mad idea."

Morgan snorted. "Can't always be you two that come up with the clever stuff..."

"Let's see... maybe I don't need a full shift. Maybe just a hand." Cameron rolled his sleeve and waggled his fingers experimentally. "Can I do that?" He shut his eyes, remembering how recently those same fingers had been shaped entirely differently. He saw the paw in his mind, covered in dense black hair, each pad a soft sheath for a strong retractable claw...

A wolf paw swiped the lock, swatting it to the ground as easily as you might bat away a fly.

He flexed his claws. Fur retreated beneath his skin, his talons shrank and his paw rippled back into being a human hand.

"That. Was. Awesome!" breathed Morgan.

"It was, wasn't it?" Cameron allowed himself a grin.

"Do you think I should've tried for a tail as well?"

"Whatever works for you."

"Maybe not right now. You know, I'm just worried it's all getting a bit too easy."

"Smart person problems. Only *you* could worry about that. Try not overthinking, just act." Morgan pulled the gate open. It swung towards him a little too fast and stotted off his head.

Cameron stifled a yelp. "Good advice. I'll remember that."

Morgan gave him a dark look and made a sub-vocal growl. "Whatever..."

They moved along the passageway, past windows showing stones covered in geodesic pictish symbols. A fire exit was being held ever-so-slightly ajar by the presence of a foot in a pointed shoe.

"What's taken you so long?" Eve hissed. "They think I'm on a bathroom break, but I've already been gone half an hour. Someone might notice." She ushered the boys quickly into the darkened gallery.

"They're all upstairs sipping drinks in the main hall, wandering around and being catty about each others' research... Some bald Professor came up to me and asked what I thought about Black's paper. 'Young Black's either going to change our understanding of the world or he's going to break it, and I don't approve of either,' he said, then he stared at me like he expected an answer..."

"Eek," said Cameron. "How did you escape?"

"I said I was Black's sister and I made pottery owls

for a living and he harrumphed and let me go... But I got the impression they all think his ideas are pretty controversial."

"Pottery owls!" Cameron gave a half-smile. "What about Dr Black and Mr Grey? Any sign?"

"Not yet. I think Black's planning to make his big entrance later..."

"It's spooky down here," said Cameron, glancing round the basement gallery at the carved stones, broken helmets, skulls and bones.

"It's full of old dead things... What did you expect?" Morgan pushed his nose against the glass of a display case. Lying on a backdrop of roots was a thin female wooden figure with beaded eyes. "Most of this stuff must date back to before the Parallel was even formed..."

"Don't!" Eve caught his arm and pulled him away. "Hey, what's up?"

"It may be old, but I don't think it's all dead." She lowered her eyes for a second. "I had a quick look about on the Parallel while I was waiting, just in case I could see Black's World Engine... and that thing spoke. It said in a high reedy voice, 'Are you the girl who brings me leaves and flowers? Is it time to rise?' I told her it was night and she should go back to sleep." Eve shivered. "I think we should tread carefully. Be respectful. We don't know what we might wake up."

"She's right. Doesn't that look familiar?" Cameron paused to examine a Roman statue of a lioness that had been dredged up from under the water. Centuries

227

of erosion had eaten away its features, but it reminded him uncomfortably of Janus's feline stationmaster. "Let sleeping relics lie, I reckon. Do you know where Black's giving his speech?"

"In the science galleries. I'll show you."

Eve led the way up the stairs that rose into the main section of the museum. The light levels increased as they approached the central hall, as did the hubbub of voices. They passed into a large gallery with two balconies ringed around a central space filled with icons of innovation and engineering.

Cameron found himself lingering, staring up at a majestic metal rocket that towered above him, nearly reaching the roof. Almost as tall was the giant cogged wheels and tilting wooden beam of the early industrial-age pumping mechanism next to it. At ground level, the conical shape of a NASA space capsule glinted beside a case in which the glassy-eyed remains of Dolly – the world's first cloned sheep – rotated. An open doorway gave onto the area holding the evening reception, which was thronged with people in smart clothes, all milling and chatting.

"Baa," Morgan said solemnly to the stuffed sheep.

"No, Morgan. Just no," said Eve. "That isn't helping."

"What? You said we had to be respectful."

"I didn't mean to –" She broke off as a bald-headed man in a dinner jacket left the party and came bustling up to her.

"Ah, there you are, my dear. I was wondering if you'd got lost? This is an unusual conference venue, but not without its amusements."

"Hello Professor Babbage. How... nice to see you again." Eve made frantic flicking motions behind her back, indicating Cameron and Morgan should take cover, but it was too late.

The Professor frowned. "Who are your friends?"

"Students," said Eve.

"Remarkably scruffy, even for our lot." Professor Babbage scrutinised Cameron's muddy trainers and Morgan's leather jacket. "And surprisingly young?"

"We're boy geniuses," said Morgan.

"Genii," corrected Cameron, shooting his friend a stare. "Dr Morgan here got his PhD in, uh, moon studies when he was just fifteen. Isn't that right?"

"Oh yeah. Know everything about Her Fat Moon ness. You could say I'm a fan." Morgan grinned.

"Is that so?" The Professor raised an eyebrow. "Perhaps then your combined intellect could help me solve a little mystery? You see, I was speaking with the esteemed Dr Black, and I mentioned I'd had the pleasure earlier of conversing with his sister – and do you know what he said?"

"It wasn't a pleasure?" said Eve brightly.

"He tells me he's an only child. He was quite insistent on the point. I can only conclude therefore that you're here without permission." Professor Babbage's eyes became small and weasely. "What are you – Press? Industry? Some interloper from an upstart university?

229

I might forgive that, under some circumstances... or I might just call security."

"Security at a boffin conference..." Morgan looked bored. "How scary can that be? C'mon Eve, never mind this creep."

"You're no students." The Professor flushed red. "And you'll find museum security is quite adept at tackling louts." He raised his voice. "In here! Intruders! Trying to damage the collection! Come quickly!"

"World-shift!" yelled Cameron. "Slip to the Parallel!"

"Oh, what a good idea," said Eve.

"Works for me," added Morgan.

The Professor faded. Cameron had time to see his expression change from outrage to bemusement before the Human World was lost from view. He wouldn't normally have advocated a world-shift when it could be observed, but, thought Cameron, the old man deserved it...

He took in his new surroundings.

The Parallel version of the room retained the same arched roof and circling balconies, but was free of all the exhibits – apart from one. The vintage Industrial Age pumping mechanism had grown, its interlocking wheels and pistons spreading to cover one side of the hall. A railing surrounded the bulky contraption, below which its lower parts vanished into the ground. From the machine's centre, two huge cantilevered arms projected in both directions, a globe mounted at each extremity. On the left-hand sphere, tiny white clouds on wires hovered over a blue sea, and Cameron recognised the familiar continents of Earth. By contrast, its counterpart on the right was predominantly red, its landmasses dark and ragged. It, he deduced, must represent Daemonic.

"The World Engine," he breathed. "It's got to be."

Beneath the projecting arms – and connected to them by cogs – a vertical screw ran to the top plate of an open cylindrical space. Inside the tall chamber, a scrap of something black shifted: an empty void that made his eyes ache.

He moved closer. The darkness twisted and turned. Every time it approached the limits of the chamber an arc of brilliant blue light flashed, forcing it back to the centre. Somehow, it made him think of a wild animal in a trap – caught by its leg and trying desperately to escape.

How-ooooo-ooooooo-ooooooooo-l!

He cried out, fingers digging into his temples. The wolf howl had never sounded louder or more urgent in his head. Eve and Morgan rushed to his side.

"I'm ok," he managed to say as the howl died away. "The Engine's been anchored to the heart of the Parallel, I can feel it. It knows it's gonna be torn apart. I can't let that happen." His face crumpled. "What do I do?"

"You know." Eve's voice was quiet. "You've already been told. You give up the wolf. You have to let it go."

"What does that even mean?" Cameron yelled,

turning on her. "I wouldn't know how to. I don't know what to do!"

"Hush up, you two," Morgan frowned, his head cocked. "There's one thing I don't understand –"

"Only one thing? Are you sure?" Eve snapped. She put a hand to her mouth. "Sorry. Nervous again, would you believe?"

"You're forgiven. I was gonna say – that lump of metal's not moving. So why the noise? Where's the steam coming from?"

Cameron's eyes met Morgan's. A wheeze haunted the room, like the breath of a sleeping giant. He reached out, fingers spread to touch the blackened metal of the machine's main wheel. "He's right. It's cold... There's no vibration."

Morgan moved to the railings and peered over. A fug of smoke nestled thick around the engine's foundations. "Seems to be coming from below." He ducked down, stuck his head through the bottom rungs and waved his arms, trying to clear the steam. "There's definitely something moving down there..."

"That would be me." A metal hand telescoped out of the smog and anchored itself around Morgan's neck. The boy retched and kicked, his face turning red. He clawed at the pincers. Cameron and Eve rushed forward, trying to prise the hand away, but it held fast.

"Grab his legs, Eve! Don't let it drag him through!"

Without stopping to think, Cameron vaulted over the edge at the unseen assailant. His feet hit ground

– just a couple of metres down – and he choked as the foul air entered his lungs. A single orange eye glowed malevolently at him through the fog.

As his vision adjusted to the smoke, he realised he was staring at the cannibalised remains of Watt... The mechanical man was in a sorry state compared to his appearance back in Hogg's chambers. His body parts and innards were dispersed, a latticework of wires and spot-welds connecting them in to the Engine. His chest inspection-port hung wide, exposing his padlock-shaped heart valve.

"I've waited years for this. I've sacrificed everything." Tiny intricate gears spun and bellows pumped, visible within the stripped-down robot's skull. "I – *WE* will not be stopped."

The pistons in Watt's one remaining arm hissed. Methodically, his metallic fingers began to squeeze the life out of Morgan.

CHAPTER 19
DOOMSDAY ENGINE

Cameron roared. Instinctively, his hands became wolf paws and he swiped at Watt's chest, trying to claw apart the mechanism that powered the robot. Sparks flew as nails struck metal.

Watt's disembodied head ratcheted round. "The wolf is strong," he observed impassively, continuing to throttle Morgan. "Machinery is stronger."

"Can't – breathe!" Morgan gasped, tearing at the pincers.

"Cameron, he's slipping through! I can't hold him," Eve shouted. "Do something!"

The robot's telescoping arm contracted, pulling Morgan closer. The boy's arms jerked, becoming progressively more uncoordinated, then he fell limp, as if he had no more fight left. As Cameron watched, helpless, something small and brassy slipped from inside Morgan's shirt and swung down, clanking against hard metal.

Get to the heart of the mystery...

Cameron's eyes sharpened. He grabbed the Omniclavis, snapping the cord from Morgan's neck. It slipped from his grasp and clinked to the ground.

Hands! he thought desperately *Be human again!* I need accuracy now, not power.

Pink human fingers plucked the key from the oily floor. He turned and slammed it into the centre of Watt's heart valve, twisting sharply. The valve popped open as the key morphed to fit, and a bright arc shot between the separate halves. Electrical crackles seethed, crawling like lightning bugs over the network of Watt's interconnected body parts.

"Sparkles!" Cameron whooped. "At last!"

With a hiss of escaping pressure, Watt's fingers sprang apart and his arm collapsed, falling in on itself, tier by tier. Cameron grabbed Morgan's shoulders, catching him before he could topple headfirst into the pit. The wolf-boy's eyelids fluttered weakly in response, and Cameron let out a long breath. "I've got you, mate – I've got you." Suddenly, he found himself supporting the full load of a semi-conscious Morgan. "Why do you weigh so much?"

He shouted up to Eve, "He's free! It's ok! Watch out, I'm sending him back –" He pushed, propelling Morgan through the rungs, to the relative safety of the gallery floor.

"You – have – achieved – nothing." Watt's eye was

dimming, his voice slurring and winding down.

"Oh yeah?" Cameron brushed his hands on his jeans. "I put a stop to you. That's something."

"In – destruction – I am – complete. As – my – motor – enters – its – last – cycle, the – engine –"

The rhythmic wheeze of Watt's mechanism stuttered, and the smoke in the pit began to thin and clear. As his final gasp faded and his eye-light went dark, a deeper rumble was heard. Heavy bass notes vibrated the bones in Cameron's chest, and the ground beneath him seemed to tremble in sympathy.

The World Engine was coming to life...

Hurriedly, Cameron leapt and grabbed the base of the railings, his trainers scuffing against the brick wall of the inspection pit as he scrambled his way out. "Watt's been shut down – no reboot for him – but we've got bigger problems..."

Eve was strangely quiet, he thought, as he levered himself out between the rungs. He registered Morgan: propped up, back against a control panel, his eyes half-open and dazed. Eve stood by him, her arms pressed tight to her sides, her face an ashen white. Cameron started to ask if they were all right – then a sickly smell of sugary mushrooms flooded his senses, and a damp hand took hold of the scruff of his neck.

"How kind of you to help us. These ancient mechanisms can be so hard to get going, but you've given us a kick start." Mr Grey hauled a struggling Cameron to his feet. "Now, be reasonable... Even a headstrong whelp like you must recognise when he is outnumbered."

His podgy arm gestured to the hall. Lumbering out of the shadows came eight of Grey's half-formed clones. At the head of the formation strode a smart-suited figure: Dr Black, a smile upon his thin face. The squad of Grey men took up positions around the engine. Two staggered over to guard Eve and Morgan, their distorted features leering.

"Any wolfish outbursts, and your friends will suffer," Grey purred in Cameron's ear. "I have merely to think the command, and they will be *ended*. Snuffed out! Do you understand?"

Cameron eyed the lurching, shambling blob-men with disgust. "Someone call Egyptology, I think there's been a break out. It's like Attack of the Zombie Mummies in here." He shot a look of pure hatred at Dr Black. "Complete with mad Professor."

"It's too late for jokes, Cam," Eve whispered. She bit her lip.

"Don't say that. It's never too late to laugh at people like him –"

"I will have respect, sir!" Grey shook Cameron hard by the collar. Cameron aimed a retaliatory elbow at Grey's ribs, but the momentum of the jab was lost within the folds of Grey's skin. It was like trying to punch a sack of dough.

"The girl's right. It's time for this childish interference to end." Dr Black moved to the control panel of the World Engine and studied the rows of twitching dials with satisfaction. "You caused Professor Babbage to have a seizure, did you know that?"

"Good," said Eve. "Nasty old man."

"I would worry how my reputation might be affected by your little vanishing act, but by the end of the evening I think the conference will have other concerns..." Black delivered a sharp rap to a gauge. The indicator needle within was progressing towards the end of a green zone. His look of satisfaction increased. "Pressure building nicely. Soon I'll be able to engage the dimensional compressor." He depressed a lever, and the twin globes at the ends of the World Engine's arms began to revolve. The bass rumble increased in intensity.

"I don't get why you're doing this," Cameron said through gritted teeth. "What's the purpose? Why wipe out the Parallel?"

"It stands in my way. It was never meant to exist."

"But what you're attempting is crazy dangerous – don't you see? Even Mitchell and Astredo – two of the greatest mages ever – couldn't entirely split the worlds. What makes you think this overgrown steam train can do it?"

Dr Black froze at the controls. His back twitched. "Did I hear you correctly? Is that what you believe is happening? That I'm attempting to complete the World Split?"

"Why do you think we're fighting? If this heap of junk – this doomsday machine – goes wrong, who knows what'll happen! The Parallel's a fault line: damage it and you could destroy everything – the Human and the Daemon Worlds as well!"

Dr Black turned round and laughed. "'Doomsday

machine' is apt, but the rest of what you say is quite wrong." He gestured proudly to the Engine. "Do you realise who designed this?"

"The Makaris, but –"

"And who were they, and what happened to them? Come on, answer the question." Dr Black's tone was condescending, like a teacher who believed an otherwise bright pupil was somehow failing him.

"A clan of daemons that lived off human life energy." Cameron glowered. "They died because the World Split locked them to Daemonic, and they couldn't reach any more people to feed off, but –"

"Precisely." Black held up a finger. "That was their doomsday – and this machine was the solution! The World Engine was a last desperate attempt to reverse the damage caused by Mitchell and Astredo's failed experiment. The last Makaris starved before it could be completed. But I – Dr Black – have recovered it, reconstructed it, and now it shall be set in motion..."

Black threw a series of switches with all the swagger of a concert pianist approaching the final triumphant moments of his performance. A thud shook the gallery, and the arms of the machine juddered. The giant wheel of the Engine began to rotate, spinning with increasing speed.

"In operation, the World Engine has an elegant simplicity." Black spoke over the rising machine tone, gesturing to a point high above them on the ceiling. "As the twin globes rise and approach their apogee, Parallel matter is simultaneously compressed and destroyed. At the point when the two globes meet, the World Split will be over."

"*Over?* Hold on... You're telling me... We've got it backwards?" Cameron felt weak inside, as if he would've fallen had Grey's clammy fingers not been holding him up. "You're not trying to separate the worlds, to finish the World Split – *you're bringing them back together?*"

"Of course." Black was exultant. "After three hundred years, the natural order of things will be restored."

"But you can't! It'd be suicide!"

"It is science."

"Don't you realise what'll happen? All the mythical creatures that used to cross over into the Human World – all the old daemons and monsters that once preyed on mankind – they'll all come back! The bottleneck of the Parallel is all that's holding them – and you're destroying it. *You're opening the floodgates*!"

"Not my concern," said Black mildly.

"It'll cause chaos!" said Cameron. "Human life as we know it will be over!"

"He's right!" Eve interjected, wrestling with the Grey who restrained her. "The Human World isn't ready for daemons any more."

"I'm putting things back as they should be. I can't help any minor supernatural side-effects."

"But why?" Cameron yelled. Far above him, on the roof of the gallery, heavy raindrops began to batter at the panelling. The crash of an approaching storm joined in with the rising pitch of the World Engine.

"To prove myself right, of course! Why else?" Black snarled, throwing home the final lever on the control panel. Cogs meshed with a crunch, and the giant wheel's motion was transferred to drive the mechanism. Creaking and groaning, the beams carrying the Human and Daemon globes began to rise, like hands of a clock slowly creeping to midnight. Simultaneously, the top plate of the central chamber began to descend, inch by inch, pressing down upon its dark contents.

As the Parallel matter inside thrashed and twisted, Cameron screamed – a hoarse yell of anger and pain. In his mind, his cry mingled with the howl of the wolf...

"Oh, and there was one more reason. A goal of mine. What was it, Mr Grey?" Black paused, looking momentarily confused. Then Grey's voice spoke – as moist and sickening as an over-rich plum pudding – and Dr Black's lips joined in, in perfect synchronisation: "Why, to *expand*..."

"He's cracked," Morgan said hoarsely. He groaned and rubbed his face, like he was coming back to his senses at last. He tried to drag himself to his feet, but a blob-man grabbed him and shoved him roughly back down. "No one sane could start this."

"Funny you should say that, werewolf," said Black. "Do you know what began my quest – the single event that set me on the path to greatness?"

"You were dropped on your head? Repeatedly?"

Dr Black hunkered down before Morgan. He held his face inches away from the teenager's, meeting his defiant stare. "I saw a boy turn into a wolf-cub..."

CHAPTER 20

DAEMONSTRABLE
EVIDENCE

As the speed of the Engine's wheel increased and the Parallel matter compressed, there was an aching sensation in Cameron's chest – like something vital was being pulled from him. But indignation overcame pain. "Come on, Black. I've seen a werewolf change and it didn't make me into a psychopath. It's *awesome*. Best thing ever –"

Dr Black's face turned pinched, and his hands clenched. "You over-privileged little brats. Born to the Great Families of the Parallel, I bet it was all handed to you on a plate: the hidden history of the worlds, your power and your right to shift between them..."

Cameron choked out a mirthless laugh. "If you think I had it easy 'cause I'm Isobel Ives' grandson, you don't know anything."

"And I grew up with a Weaver Daemon, and that was no privilege. It means I know exactly the sort of terrible things you're letting back into this world." Eve shot a hard look at Mr Grey, who smiled as if she'd paid him a compliment.

"That's not important." Black straightened and ran his hands through his thinning hair. "All my life I *knew* there was something being hidden from me – some secret just out of reach. That's why I became an astronomer. I thought the answer must be out there, among the stars. My PhD was about the search for dark matter, looking for evidence of the missing mass that would explain how the universe worked. Turns out I was looking in the wrong direction. And it was the wolf-cub who showed me the way...

"One night at Blackford Observatory, while waiting to use the telescope, I saw a boy transform on the hill outside, right before my eyes. Another man might've doubted what he'd seen, but I knew what it meant. The world was even more complicated than I'd ever dared dream."

Dr Black began to pace back and forth, his hands gesticulating. It was the liveliest Cameron had ever seen the drab man.

"My research turned to the occult. I would find a way of understanding that wolf transformation! Deep in the university vaults, I uncovered the papers of Alexander Mitchell. He was a geologist as well as a mage, did you know that? He studied the formation of the Earth, deducing historical process from the craggy rocks of Arthur's Seat...

"None of my colleagues had ever thought to look into the rest of his writings. They dismissed his arcane work as superstition. But I went through his legacy, and there I discovered the World Split, and the true nature of the dual worlds. The secret of the universe, laid out on damp and crumbling pages..."

Dr Black gazed up reverentially at the two revolving globes creeping ever closer. He turned back to the teenagers, his arms spread wide. "Don't you see? It's all connected: my quest for secrets, the stars, the wolf... *The Daemon World provides the explanation for dark matter!* The cosmos – as human astronomers perceive it – omits the Earth's daemonic twin, because they simply don't know it's there. But logically, if the Earth has a twin, so must other planets... Many, many worlds must exist in hidden dimensions. By understanding this world – I solved the problems of physics!" Black stopped his frenzied pacing and for a moment looked much older than his years. "I explained my theories to my superiors at the University, and do you know what they said?"

"They laughed at poor Dr Black," said Mr Grey with oily sympathy. "They said he'd been overworking and needed a holiday."

"I decided to show them for the fools they were," said Black.

"Bad choice," said Morgan. "Should've taken the holiday."

Black ignored him, pressing on, driven by a burning need to share his story, even with his enemies. "By now my own connection to the Parallel had become clear. I carried the Parallel Inheritance within me, even if its knowledge had been lost to my family. It was the reason I'd always felt different, the reason I knew there was something hidden..."

"That's one theory," Morgan muttered darkly. "Or you got dropped on your head."

Again Black ignored him. "So I made a plan. I would learn to world-shift myself. I'd leave this world and bring back something that'd show them – that'd prove them all wrong."

Cameron swallowed. All his life, he'd known that feeling of difference Dr Black described. When the Parallel had first opened up with a rush of music, part of him had changed forever. He had felt a rush of excitement – and the sense of something missing, at long last returned. "How did you do it? How did you get to the Parallel?"

"Numbers! Beautiful equations. As a student I would walk about the city, and numbers would dance inside my head. I'd look up and find myself some place else entirely. People said I was absent-minded, but really it was the start of a world-shift. All I had to do was refine it, find the precise equation to focus on..." The enthusiasm drained from Dr Black's face, and his mouth twisted, like he was remembering the taste of something repellent. "I went too far. I had no one to stop me, you see? I didn't end up in the

Parallel, I transferred through to Daemonic and that's where I got... that's where I found..."

"That's where he found me." Grey's mushroom breath was warm on Cameron's neck, his wattle-like chin grazing his ear. The boy squirmed in revulsion. "I'd been locked away for ever so long... The daemons knew what I was – what I was capable of becoming. The 'Grey Death' they called me, the fungus that seeks to consume, the root of all evil..."

"Grey's what you brought back," Eve whispered, looking away. "Oh, you poor, poor man."

Dr Black's eyes went distant. "He was so small then, like a baby: a mewling, speechless thing..."

"I didn't stay silent long, did I? I was hungry. I absorbed what I needed."

"I gave him voice – and he took from me the power to leave that place."

A wave of nausea hit Cameron. *The wolf had known.* On some instinctual level he'd felt the Greys were wrong, that they didn't belong. The wolf had understood the truth.

"This fat amoeba's not even supposed to be on the Parallel, let alone the Human World." Cameron struggled against Grey's clammy hold. *"Black – what've you let out?"*

The wheel of the World Engine spun faster and the rumble increased, as if the machinery was stepping up a gear. The arms lifted, and the compression chamber closed, and Cameron cried out again.

"Hush now, hush." Grey clapped a hand over Cameron's mouth. Gorge rose in the boy's throat. Inside his head, the wolf was restless. He could feel it, yearning to break free, to tempt him into shifting, no matter what the consequences.

At full power he could get free from this overgrown bogeyman, *he could rip him apart...*

But dare he, with his friends under threat?

"That wasn't the way of it... Mr Grey helped me," said Dr Black, but his tone was uncertain. "He led me to Watt, and in turn we discovered the remains of the World Engine. We put it back together, sourcing parts and removing interference, coaxing it back to life. Anything I've needed, Grey's provided..."

"Anything in the way has been absorbed," Grey added, with relish.

"And now, with my blinkered colleagues gathered in the hall of the Human World outside, it is time to show them I was right..."

"They'll have a bunch of hungry daemons ripping off their heads," said Morgan contemptuously, "as soon as the worlds reconnect. They're not gonna live long enough to crown you King Professor."

"That would still be proof, wouldn't it, of a sort? That'd be demonstrable evidence." Black turned to the controls of the World Engine, stifling a brittle giggle. "Let them tell me to take a holiday now..."

"You really believe that's why you're doing this, don't you?" Eve dodged round her guard and threw herself at Dr Black, trying to pull him away from the levers. "It's Grey, planting ideas in your head. That's what daemons do! You've got to fight him. You can't let him take over!"

Morgan ran to join her, but what the Greys lacked in speed, they made up for in strength. The blob-men closed in around Black in a protective circle, their bulky bodies cutting off Eve and Morgan, forcing them back.

"It's no good. What do we do?" Eve shouted. *"Cam!"*

Held in the arms of the odious Mr Grey, Cameron was bent almost double, his hands clutching his chest as he convulsed. The longer the World Engine ran, the stranger he felt. Waves of energy were slamming through his body: one moment he'd never been so alive, so full of unleashed power – the next he was so feeble that if Grey had released him, he would've toppled to the ground.

The Engine's compression chamber was now only a fraction of the size it had been when the mechanism started. The twin arms rose, approaching midnight, the globes spinning so fast their outlines seemed to blur.

"First the chaos, then the feast. Two whole worlds for me to absorb," Mr Grey oozed, drool running down his pasty chin. "A new dawn is coming, and all shall be Grey."

"And I will be proved right," said Dr Black.

"The globes!" Eve screamed. *"Look – they're touching!"*

The gallery rocked to a sound like a supersonic boom. Shaken loose by the colossal vibration, a glass ceiling panel dropped and shattered, scattering a million tiny daggers across the floor.

The sky beyond was red and bruised, roiling with black thunderclouds.

Cameron shut his eyes.

CHAPTER 21

HOWL

Black paws on white snow...

The ground beneath your pads is hard and crisp.

Easy to slip on, so claws spread wide, but it's firmer than the deeper drifts – more of a kickback from your hind legs – so you can go swift.

Ears twitch, eyes scan: left to right, down to the ground, then back to the horizon.

Human boy in front of you. His dark, almost black hair hangs low on his forehead, shielding his expression, but you scent-see him – know him – instantly.

Cameron.

He is you – but *you are not him.*

Not any longer.

Brown eyes meet yours, questioning.

"This is it, isn't it? This is when I let you go."

You hold his gaze. Wolves don't speak or give approval. They just act. They just are.

He understands this. It is, after all, part of wolves' beauty.

You settle on your haunches and you throw back your head and howl: a long, resonant cry that echoes across the daemonic forest.

The boy recalls something Morgan told him, back when you were new-formed, just a speck of wolf-blood mingled with Parallel magic: 'You howl for the things you need, and you howl for the things you can't have... Sometimes you can't tell what sort of howl it's gonna be. Not till you've let it out."

This is a howl of need.

Out of the darkness, surging, running, come wolves of every size and hue. Pelts of grey, black, brindled brown and white. They race forward and past you, leaping and yipping and snapping. Processing in the wake of the wild hunt, carrying staffs of oak, come the Wolf King and Queen. They walk upright, in human form. They bow to you and to Cameron in turn.

"Your pack has come at the time of greatest need," says the Wolf Queen, "as we promised."

The Wolf King's brow is as black as night. "The Daemon and the Human World touch. We too may be wolves in either place."

"Black seeks to reunite the Worlds forever. The Parallel is dying," the boy speaks bluntly, "and if you let it, the danger threatens not just the humans, but the pack as well. Your precious isolation will be gone.

The Grey death will spread everywhere, even over the forest. You must stop him."

The King and Queen nod their obedience. The pair pass onwards, following the pack towards a reddish light glowing beyond the trees.

You are alone once more.

Just you – and the boy that was also you.

"I was told this had to happen. I didn't believe it. I didn't want it. I still don't." He screws up his eyes and stares at you, a look of intense determination. "But if it saves the Parallel, if it saves Morgan and Eve, if it stops Grey – then I choose it. I choose to set you free."

You walk forward and touch your nose to his hand, a gesture of parting.

Cameron shuts his eyes and he throws back his head, and howls – howls with his human voice. It is musical; and in its cadences, you recognise the song of the Parallel.

The music that is part of you both, and lives inside, and always will... no matter what.

You shut your eyes and you howl too.

You both know what sort of howl it is.

It is the howl for the things you can't have.

It is a howl of loss.

CHAPTER 22

WOLF AGAINST
THE MACHINE

Cameron opened his eyes. His head thrashed from side to side, and broke free from Grey's smothering hands. He yelled at the top of his voice, howling with such ferocity that his cry soared over the roar of machinery, and even the great wheel of the Engine appeared to falter in its spin.

"Pathetic." Grey swiped drool from his chin and moved to stare Cameron in the eye. "What a sad display. Do you hear, Dr Black, how the boy wails his defeat?"

"Defeat?" Morgan broke into a broad grin. "Can tell you don't speak wolf... That ain't a call of bad times, that's summoning up the pack. The word you're searching for is *reinforcements*."

Hope leapt on Eve's face. She danced on the spot,

jigging round a suspicious Grey that swiped idly at her. "Is it true? Are they coming?"

"I know it," said Cameron. "I saw them. They're on their way."

"Who? What's he talking about, Grey?" Dr Black worked the World Engine controls furiously. "We're so close to success – nothing can be allowed to go wrong."

The gallery was shaking. Around its edges, patches of the walls were becoming indistinct, letting in hints of the livid red sky and darkened landscape of the Daemon World. Two of the pillars that held up the vaulted roof were taking on the appearance of towering pine trees, beyond which Cameron could glimpse a tangled snow-covered forest. Leather-black creatures swooped in the air like predatory kites, and he could hear the rustle of movement as things unseen stalked through the undergrowth.

The patches of instability grew and spread together like ink blots as the Daemon World came closer. Meanwhile, through the archway that led to the museum's main hall, the ghostly outlines of the conference guests could be seen moving about, their agitation suggesting the changes wrought here were starting to reach the Human World as well. In the very centre of the gallery, at the heart of it all, the World Engine churned and hammered as its globes spun and the Parallel contracted and the two opposing realities were drawn together. Wreathed in clouds of smoke and steam, its ironwork was framed against the stark red backdrop of the largest patch of instability of all.

"The boy's bluffing," Grey spat, his milky eyes scouring the room. "The Parallel around the World Split fault-line was cleared. There's no help coming, no boundary-crossers left to interfere."

"Oh no? Try the forests of Daemonic..." Cameron's gaze was fixed on the trees that were becoming ever more solid. He could sense the vibration of hundreds of feet, running on all fours towards them. "Because look out – *here comes the pack!*"

He darted forward, grabbing both Eve and Morgan and pulling them towards the railings that surrounded the Engine, motioning them to climb to the top rung. As they did so, the wolves came thundering into the room, bursting from between the tree-pillars and turning the gallery floor into a sea of fur. The wolves ran at the Greys, snarling, snapping and biting. The blobby clones of Mr Grey retaliated, swinging their puffball arms, which connected with their attackers with wet and sickening thuds. Hanks of fur flew and the air filled with yowls as the Greys' lifted away wolf-sharp teeth, eyes and claws, absorbing the matter into themselves, and growing fatter still.

"*Forget the blobs!* You've gotta go for him – he's the root," Morgan roared, gesturing at Mr Grey who hissed in alarm. "Take him out, and they'll all go down." The wolf-boy rolled his eyes, pulling his jacket from his shoulders, his arms already stretching and thickening. "Want a job done..."

He launched into the wolvish melee with a whoop. For a moment, the blond teenager seemed to be crowdsurfing, then he shifted completely into his white wolf form and dropped into the crowd.

"Don't join in." Eve's arm bracketed protectively across Cameron's chest. "I know you want to, but don't. I can't lose you both –"

"It's not up to me." The boy's breath was ragged, the sweat pouring down his face. "*He'll* know when to come. It's got to be soon."

The white wolf pushed to the front of the pack, leading his colleagues in a charge towards Mr Grey. The daemon stumbled, driven back by sheer force of numbers. He backed closer and closer towards the heart of the World Engine.

"Morgan! The compression chamber," Cameron gasped, "get Grey into its field. Don't let him expand..."

"No..." Eve gave a yell of excitement. "*Make him contract!*"

The wolf-tide surged and Grey retreated. He teetered on the threshold of the chamber, his podgy hands batting at the snapping muzzles, then, with a ghastly cry, he toppled backward. There was a brilliant blue flash. For a moment he appeared wedged in the compression field, elephantine and furious, then the machine gave a laboured groan. There was a thin, high-pitched sound like gas escaping from a punctured weather balloon, and Mr Grey *dwindled*. He shrunk first to the size of a beachball, then a puffball, then finally – to nothing at all.

All round the gallery, his spored minions froze. They withered and collapsed, falling in on themselves like sacks of wet leaves dropping mushily to the floor. Soon the only thing left was a manky grey paste, trampled under the paws of the stampeding pack.

"No more old mushroom breath," said Eve with satisfaction. She shot a look in the direction of Dr Black. "But I don't think doomsday's cancelled yet…"

The scientist's attention was focussed entirely on the operating panel of the World Engine. If the disposal of his controlling colleague had affected him, he didn't show it – he just kept tapping dials and working levers.

"Give it up, Black," panted Cameron, climbing down from the railings. A large white wolf pushed boisterously to Cameron's side and he absently patted its flank in greeting. With the threat of the Greys gone, the pack was calming – the wolves parting to allow Cameron and wolf-Morgan through to confront Black.

"Grey's gone. You don't need to do this any more," said Cameron. "And my wingmen agree." From behind him, many pairs of green eyes glowered at the human scientist.

Black did not look up. "I'm so close now, so close to my life's goal…"

"Grey flesh has soured wolvish tongues. They taste

of must and decay, and are ill-digested," the Wolf King announced as he and the Queen entered the gallery, striding through from the patch of shifting dimensions. "The pack may savour the taste of something fresher." His words were underscored by a bass rumble – a collective growl from the wolves that made the threat very clear.

Dr Black turned round. His eyes went wide at the sight of the Queen. "The fair-haired woman... the wolf mother. You were there at the start – on Blackford Hill. You're a sign, surely – a symbol that my experiment has to succeed?"

"No." The Wolf Queen's fingers touched the circlet on her brow. "This is the only symbol I carry. And it isn't intended for you." She moved through the horde of wolves and placed the circlet over Morgan's head. He resisted for a moment as she slipped it to rest like a silver collar on the ruff of fur round his neck. "Your twisted philosophy threatens us all, Dr Black. It can't be allowed to continue."

"Then there's nothing else to do." Black's face drained of colour. "I will have my victory, even if I'm not here to see it." He snapped a final lever down on the Engine. "It's finished. The mechanism is locked and it can't be shut off until the worlds synchronise and the final particle of Parallel is destroyed." He stepped away from the control panel and started to climb up the iron framework of the pounding Engine, on to the top plate of the compression chamber. He held his hands aloft to the swirling red bruise of the daemonic sky. For a moment he stood silhouetted as he swayed giddily on the spot.

Eve shouted a warning. "Look out. He's going to –"

A black-winged shape swooped through the vortex. Powerful claws punctured Black's shoulders, seizing him and lifting him up.

"Proof," he breathed. "At last."

A razor-sharp beak clacked. Black gave a gargling scream that choked off as he was snatched back through to the Daemon World.

"Food for a Tantalus daemon." The Wolf King laughed. "Better it than us. He would've stuck in my craw."

"Never mind menu suggestions," Eve yelled. "What about the machine? How are we going to stop it?"

The two arms of the Engine were overlapping, the spinning globes merging in a blur of light. The archway to the main hall showed the Human World ever more distinctly. People were running – fleeing for their lives from the shaking building.

Eve turned to Cameron. The boy was staring transfixed at the central wheel of the machine. His first howl had rocked it – disturbed it somehow – the vibration throwing it out of kilter. "The Augur was right. Music might be my salvation, after all..."

He shouted to the massed pack, "Wolves! Brothers and sisters! Were-people with a face for Human and Daemon worlds alike – you're creatures of both, no matter what you've been taught. If you've ever loved either World, then *howl now*, I command you."

Green eyes turned obediently towards him.

"Direct your voice at the Engine's main wheel, and howl together. We're gonna to try to throw it out of phase, so howl with all you've got!"

He threw back his head and let loose his own cry. The wolves circled the machine, forming an arc around the mechanism, their snouts pointing towards the churning wheel, and followed his call. The air was rent with plaintive song: eerie, multiple and beautiful.

The World Engine stuttered, its mechanism reacting to the bombardment of sound waves – but still the wheel spun.

"It's not strong enough," the Wolf King snarled. "We need another voice for the quorum. We must be louder."

"We need the leader," added the Wolf Queen, between soaring cries.

The white wolf turned to look at Cameron, his ears flattened. His green eyes flashed a question.

"We need Wolf You, Cam," Eve said, putting Morgan's question into words.

Cameron nodded, holding his arms in front of him, fists clenched. "That's your cue," he said, bracing himself. "Time to go."

He stretched his mouth wide and howled again, with all his heart.

He could see the wolf fur overlaid on his arms, but it wasn't his skin sprouting and morphing as usual – the hair lay across him like a shadow. For a second he saw both – fur and human flesh together – then his howl became a scream. The fur shifted and slipped forward, the shadow moving away, out into the room. It solidified into the shape of a huge black wolf, larger and more powerfully built than any of the others. Cameron's open arms fell back and he sighed a long breath, dropping to his knees. His throat was ragged and his chest felt unnaturally light, as if there was nothing left inside of him at all.

The black form sauntered, almost casually, to the centre of the arc of wolves around the engine, sat back on its haunches and howled. A new call entered the chorus, and the cries all seemed to synchronise – becoming at last a single, perfect resonant note.

The central wheel cracked and stalled. The globes froze, and sheared free of their bearings, ricocheting like cannonballs across the gallery at ceiling height. The arms of the machine crashed down, causing the top plate of the compression chamber to fly upwards. All round the room, the red patches of instability sizzled and zipped out of existence.

With the quickest of glances back at the boy it had split from, the black wolf charged forward, leaping into the remaining fragment of Parallel matter. The two merged together and grew – and there was a brilliant flash of multicoloured light.

Cameron blacked out.

" – exploded. It doesn't make sense.... not possible... thing's just for display. It's ancient. The Boulton & Watt steam engine hasn't run on actual steam for –" A distant voice was shouting indignantly, there was the squawk of walkie-talkies, the scream of sirens, but everything was black and fuzzy, and –

When Cameron woke again, Eve was cradling his head, back in the museum's Science Hall in the Human World. The old steam pumping-engine lay shattered and smoking, the glittering space rocket was toppled and twisted. Display cases were broken, their precious contents scattered to the floor. Through a ragged and scorched hole in the roof, a persistent dreich rain fell. The sky beyond was a reassuringly Edinburgh shade of slate grey.

"It's ok," Eve spoke gently. "You did it. You stopped the World Engine."

"What about the Worlds?"

"They touched, but they didn't merge. When the Engine stopped, they moved apart again. Now it's all turning back to normal, fading away like a bad dream. I think the worst place hit was here – like being at the very centre of an explosion." She smiled sympathetically. "Are you all right?"

"I feel like..." Cameron tried to struggle into an upward position and let out a pathetic moan.

"Like you shouted out a wolf – and got blown

from the Parallel by an exploding doomsday machine?"

"That'd describe it, yeah."

"Cameron," Eve said quietly, "I don't understand. How could the wolf just split off from you like that?"

"He came from the Parallel, really – that same night Morgan's bite saved my life." Cameron thought of the wolf racing forward, leaping joyously into the void. "It's like he's been waiting all this time for the right moment to go home." His brow furrowed. "What about Morgan? Is he ok?"

"He's with the pack. Once your wolf-self vanished, they seemed to decide he was in control. He's not happy about it, but the King's gone – the Queen too. They just walked away, vanished into Daemonic..."

"I have to go see –"

"Cameron, you need to take it easy."

He shook his head. Slowly, and with great effort, he managed to stand. He closed his eyes, reaching for the Song of the Parallel in his mind. He heard the first few notes – then it stopped, died away...

He tried again.

The notes started, but he lost the rhythm almost at once. Nothing changed...

He was still here: stuck in this world, among the dust and debris and dripping rainwater.

"Eve," he whispered. "I can't world-shift. It's not working."

Eve looked away. "Maybe none of us can. We don't know how much is left of the Parallel. It might nearly all be gone, destroyed by the awful machine. Maybe that means it's impossible to world-shift –"

"I don't believe that – and you don't either," said Cameron, his jaw set. "You made it back here, and Morgan's still there, and anyway..." He paused. "I can't explain it, but I know it hasn't all disappeared."

"*We* should disappear," Eve glanced round the shattered room, "before people start asking what we're doing here, and did we have anything to do with blowing up their nice museum?"

"But Eve –"

"Cameron, you saved us," she said quietly. "Do you realise that? You saved us all. Me and Morgan and the pack –"

"I know, but – " Cameron reached for the Song of the Parallel again. A few notes sang tantalisingly in his mind, but faded before the tune kicked in. It was infuriating and sad – like knowing you'd once heard the best song *ever*, but not being able to recall more than a couple of fragments – and not being certain you'd ever hear it again.

And it wasn't just any song – it was the song that let him move between the worlds...

"*Everyone* was in danger if the Humanian and Daemonic worlds merged," Eve emphasised, "and you saved them all." She looked at her brother and smiled. "That's amazing. Isn't it enough for you?"

"I guess so. I guess it's got to be," Cameron said. But he knew in his heart that it wasn't enough at all.

CHAPTER 23

PRETTY GOOD YEAR

The sun was setting over Blackford Hill, sliding behind the turret of the Observatory and lighting the grass in a golden glow.

Cameron could feel no werewolvish urges in his body, no strange desire to stretch and quiver and change. There was just the thump of his heart, the wind in his ears and the sensation of the skin on his face tightening against the chill of a night in early spring.

Eve said he should stop coming up here, mooning about, that he was only torturing himself with what he'd lost, but he couldn't help it. It was his right to remember, wasn't it? To think about the fun he'd had, running wild, on those mad nights. It had been a pretty good year, all in all, until Black and Grey had turned up.

And besides, tonight he had someone to meet.

Stalking up the hill in great rangy strides came a figure in a long army greatcoat and biker boots, his tangled hair blowing behind him. He gave a curt nod to Cameron, and the pair stood for a while, as the sun dipped lower, and the light began to fade.

"Still nothing?" said Morgan, after a time.

"Did you expect there would be?"

"Not really. If there was still a bit of wolf in you, I'd scent it. We usually know our own."

"Oh." Cameron scuffed his trainers on the ground. "I can't hear him anymore, so I guess I knew. Doesn't make it any easier though..."

"What about the world-shift? Any better?"

"I dunno. I keep catching bits of the Parallel song, but not enough to focus on. I figure if I leave it alone, maybe it'll jump out at me suddenly."

"Leap out the cupboard and give you a scare?"

"Something like that, yeah." Cameron lifted his hand, shielding his eyes. "Thing is though, I keep hearing other songs. All sorts of them. Brand new songs I've never heard before. Bits of lyrics that would go great with them too."

"That's a good thing, right?"

Cameron nodded, a secret smile on his face. He'd loved music well before he'd ever got mixed up in the Parallel. It had always felt important to him. Even if the songs he heard in his head now couldn't shift him into another world, they still made him feel different, more alive...

"Always did want to start a band."

"What you gonna play? Lead guitar?"

"Yeah, I might do a bit of singing too."

Morgan grinned lopsidedly. "Better hand out earplugs when you gig. Last time you howled, a steam engine exploded and the worlds nearly ended."

"Maybe I'll keep that for the encore."

"What you gonna be called?"

"I dunno. Werewolf Parallel?"

"Strange name."

"Just an idea I got from somewhere." Cameron shook his head. "Doesn't have to be that. I figure when I start school again, I'll ask around. Should be able to get some people together and practise a bit, work out my songs. You remember Amy? She said she could play keyboard, but I reckon she's more drums –"

"Woah, woah. Hold up. You're going back to school? Since when?"

"Since I got a glimpse of what it'd be like if I don't." Cameron sighed. "Anyway, it might not be that bad. This is a whole new city, isn't it? Miles away from my old school and problems. Whole new me too... And Amy's moving through to Edinburgh at the start of summer, so that'll be a laugh. Eve's got me reading loads to try and catch up."

"Rather you than me, mate."

Cameron stuck his hands in his pockets. "It's not like I've got much choice, is it? Since the two partners in my business decided they've got other plans."

"Low blow." Morgan's cheeks coloured. "You *know* I never wanted to lead that lot of mongrels. Been running away from that noose around my neck for as long as I can remember." His fingers fidgeted at the collar of his coat.

"But you're still doing it."

"It's not that easy, it's just..." Morgan's mouth twitched. "They're like sheep, the pack. Need someone to follow. If it's not me, it's gonna be someone worse – someone big and dumb like Grant, or mean like Lola. Maybe I can shake 'em up a bit, before I do a vanishing act. I'm thinking the whole grow-up get-boring go-and-live-in-Daemonic needs ended." He squinted at the sky and scratched his ribs. "Mind if we walk a bit?"

"Feeling the need?"

"You know how it is." Morgan scrunched his nose.

"I remember."

They climbed for a while, moving further up the hill and away from the road that led back to the human city.

"What about old grumpy?" Morgan said. "She gonna be in your band too?"

"Don't think so. She claims she prefers opera and classical." Cameron pulled a face. "Doesn't seem feasible she's my sister, does it? Must be some kind of mix up."

"I'd ask for a refund," said Morgan, deadpan. "She's still keeping you company though, right?"

"Mainly, but she's all over the place. Some days she says she never wants to see another daemon as long as she lives, the next she's got some secret plan on the go. She won't tell me, but I think it's some mad idea to track down our mum."

Morgan's eyes widened. "Can she do that?"

"In the Augur's ordeal Mrs Ferguson told Eve that mum was 'banished', and that's not the same as dead, is it? It's a slim chance, but she might be out there somewhere. I think Eve reckons she should go look."

"What about you? Up for a new adventure?"

"I can't, can I? Not unless the world-shift comes back." Cameron shrugged, affecting a casual indifference he didn't entirely possess. The truth was, this was a problem he didn't feel ready to think about. "I've gone trying to dig up the past before, haven't I, and it didn't exactly work out."

"You found Eve. And me."

"See? Told you it was a big mistake." Cameron ducked from Morgan's playfully swung fist. "It's Eve's quest. I've got to find my own way."

They stopped at the brow of the hill. A steep path lead down the other side, snaking away into rougher countryside. Morgan took off his coat, rolling it into a ball and stowing it in a hollow tree he and Cameron had often made use of. Below he was wearing the loose woven robes of the pack; clothes designed to fall away and drop to the ground as their wearer shifted from one shape to another.

"I like your dressing gown," said Cameron with heavy sarcasm. "Very rock and roll."

"Hey, it's practical, isn't it?"

"It's a look."

Morgan shucked off his boots and added them to the stash, his bare feet dancing a jig on cold earth. "Hey, I forgot. Delivery for you." He took a medallion on a length of string from a pocket in his robe and placed it around Cameron's neck. The boy dipped his chin to look, and saw the image of a two-faced man staring back at him.

"One of Janus's white kitty-cats brought it to the hall. Grant tried to bite its ear off before he realised it was marble and chipped a tooth." Morgan grinned. "I asked kitty if there was any payment due because, you know, Janus –"

"Tricky."

"Exactly. The cat said no. It was done. Sacrifice had been made, and his master was pleased to extend protection over you and yours once more."

Cameron rubbed the ward token with his thumb. "So at least I got something out of it, eh?"

Morgan flexed his arms then his legs, stretching like an athlete preparing for a marathon, and let out a long breath. "He's still out there, you know." He shot Cameron a direct look. "Other you. I see him about the Parallel. It's like he's patrolling, keeping an eye out – not letting anything bad sneak in. Well, there's still monsters and daemons, obviously, but nothing like Grey... I don't think there'll ever be anything like him again."

"Lots of Parallel to patrol, is there?" Cameron heard his voice go tight as he fought to keep it controlled.

"Oh man, *you should see it*... It's growing back bigger and madder than ever, filling up with all kinds of wild stuff. New, different things too. It's like..." Morgan stopped abruptly. "Sorry. That was tactless, even for me."

Cameron offered a smile. "It's ok. Really. I'm glad it's coming back. That's what all this was about, wasn't it?"

"That and saving the World."

"Oh. That... I forgot. It's not like they ever said thanks."

They stood and watched as the night sky turned black and the clouds parted. There was something Cameron kept remembering, something the Augur had said. He'd told him he'd only win through by giving up that which he prized the most. He wondered what that was. Sometimes he thought it was the wolf he'd had to lose and sometimes the world-shifts – *but they could come back, right?* – or maybe... maybe it was something else altogether...

He pushed the thought away. He'd made one life on the Parallel – perhaps it was time to find another. If he really tried, with his new band and everything, maybe next year could be pretty good too...

"I'm gonna run now," said Morgan. "You coming along for a bit?"

Cameron nodded. "Always."

They set off down the hill, side by side, feet dancing from grass to shingle and back again. Air pumped through Cameron's chest as their pace increased.

"This is what it means, eh?" he said between gasps, looking to his side. "Being alive?"

Morgan was no longer there. Some distance in front of him, Cameron made out the white streak of a wolf charging across the fields. Its head was down, its legs pounding the earth with grace and precision, racing with sheer joy. And then, just at the edge of his human vision, a second shape rippled out of the darkness: a wolf of such spectral blackness that it seemed to be part of the night itself.

Cameron's feet slowed and crunched to a halt. He watched the two wolves until he could see them no longer, and then he turned to go home.

Thanks to Eleanor Collins, Lindsey Fraser, Helen Jackson and Daniela Sacerdoti for the right words at the right time; Ben, Cody, Iain, Nick, Paul and Steve for thoughts of keys and feathers; and to Russell Pugh for laughing – just occasionally – at my jokes.

Praise for Daemon Parallel

'This book is absolutely brilliant... This is a great debut book and one that will fly high into my top five reads of this year.'

MR RIPLEY'S ENCHANTED BOOKS

'Edinburgh is conjured brilliantly and beautifully here, and we can really believe in it as a place suffused by magic... I adored this novel. I really, really want it to be the first in a sequence. I want it to be a boxed set of novels that are just about falling apart with repeated rereadings. That's how much I enjoyed this first one.'

PAUL MAGRS, DOCTOR WHO WRITER

'With more twists and turns than a basilisk, and a truly exciting ending that kept me on the edge of my seat, *Daemon Parallel* gripped me throughout and made me long for a sequel.'

KIDSREADBOOKS

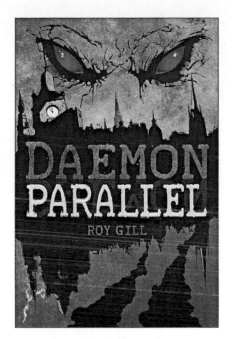

Cameron's father is dead and his inheritance is ... rather unusual.

He has the power to world-shift: travel between the Human and Daemon dimensions and the Parallel – a realm where the two worlds meet.

Between battling daemons and allying with werewolves, Cameron's new life is already pretty complicated but things are about to get even more dangerous...

 Also available as an eBook and audio book

Roy Gill was born and lives in Edinburgh. In a previous life, Roy researched media fandom at the University of Stirling but he now writes full-time and has published books for teenagers, feature-length audio drama and short fiction in several genres. He was a Scottish Book Trust New Writers Award Winner in 2010, and has been shortlisted for the Kelpies and Sceptre Prize.

The first book in his Parallel series, *Daemon Parallel*, was published in 2012 and its world-shredding sequel, *Werewolf Parallel*, appeared in 2014.

Follow him on Twitter @roy_gill and over on roygill.com